EVERYTHING BETWEEN US

HARPER BLISS

Also by Harper Bliss

Beneath the Surface
In the Distance There Is Light
No Strings Attached
The Road to You
Far from the World We Know
Seasons of Love
Release the Stars
Once in a Lifetime
At the Water's Edge
French Kissing: Season Three
French Kissing: Season Two
French Kissing: Season One
High Rise (The Complete Collection)

Copyright © 2017 Harper Bliss
Cover picture © Depositphotos / belchonock
Cover design by Caroline Manchoulas
Published by Ladylit Publishing – a division of Q.P.S. Projects Limited -
Hong Kong

ISBN-13 978-988-14910-6-0

To everyone who has ever felt like they were not enough because of how they looked. You are.

CHAPTER ONE

"I've got this one." I all but shove Micky out of the way with my behind.

"All right, all right," she says. "No need to get physical." She leans her hip against the counter, watching me—making me more nervous than I want to be for this.

"Hi," Caitlin James says on a sigh, as though ordering coffee has become a big chore, even though she gets the same thing every single day. She looks at the board above my head. I try not to stare while her gaze is fixed elsewhere, but it's hard. Although Micky scrutinizing my every move keeps me in check. "A large flat white, please," Caitlin says.

"Have here or takeaway?" I ask, out of habit.

Caitlin cocks her head and waits a beat before saying, "Have here." Her glance skitters to Micky, who is just standing there, doing nothing. "How's it going?"

"All is well on the barista front," Micky replies. It's not that long since she started working at the Pink Bean, and I was the one teasing her about having a crush on one of the regulars. Not that I have a crush on Caitlin James. Not that kind, anyway. She's too much of an icon for me to have something as mundane as a crush on.

"Still a lady of leisure?" Micky asks.

My ears perk up while I prepare Caitlin's coffee, but I can't hear what she says over the hiss of the machine steaming the milk.

"—my new neighborhood," is all I can make out from

her reply.

"Here you go." I hand Caitlin her flat white.

"Thank you." She looks me in the eye briefly, then turns her attention back to Micky. "I'll be at my usual table."

Micky and I both watch her strut to *her* table by the window.

"What was that all about?" Micky asks. "Have you got the hots for her or something?"

"No, of course not." I bring my hands to my sides. "But, you know, that's Caitlin James."

"Ha." Micky stares at me for a moment. "I take it you've read all of her books, whereas I have read zero."

"I have a couple in my bag. You can borrow them if you like." *Argh.* I could kick myself for blurting that out. I don't want Micky to borrow *my* Caitlin James books. I'll happily lend her any others, but not those.

"Why are they in your bag?"

"Just... no reason." I immediately feel put on the spot.

"Come on, Jo. You can tell me. All the time you and I spend behind this counter together. Don't you consider me a friend?"

You've certainly gotten a lot of lip since you and Robin started shagging, I want to say, but bite back. I only sigh.

"I may only be a hausfrau turned barista, but I can put two and two together." Micky keeps going. "I'm rather sharp for my age, you know?"

I wish she would just let it go.

"Since she moved to Darlinghurst, Caitlin has been coming here every day," she says.

"Would you please keep your voice down," I whisper. I feverishly wish for a customer to walk in.

"You're a *fan girl*, or whatever the kids call it these days?" She draws her lips into a pensive pout. "So you carry her books around in case..." She pushes herself away from the counter and leans toward me.

I don't give her a chance to finish her sentence. "Yes.

You sussed me out. I'm the kind of nerd who wants her books signed by the author. So what?"

"Then what are you doing standing here while she's sitting right over there?"

"I can't just go up to her and ask."

Micky raises one eyebrow. "Why not?"

"I don't know. It's disrespectful of her privacy. She came here for a cup of coffee, not to be harassed by the barista."

"Oh, come on. She'll love it. She's the type who gets off on that kind of attention."

"And you know her so well, do you?"

"What are you two whispering about?" Kristin asks.

I was so wrapped up in this ridiculous conversation, I didn't even hear her approach.

"We have a dilemma on our hands, boss," Micky says. "Perhaps you can help."

"Happy to."

Now both Kristin and Micky are staring at me. A blush creeps up my neck.

"Josephine here is a big fan of Caitlin and she wants to get some books autographed. Whatever can she do to make that happen?"

"Hm, I don't know. If only Caitlin were a regular at the Pink Bean. And a friend I've known for twenty years. These things could help, I guess. But alas," Kristin says.

I shake my head. "Once you're done mocking me, I'd like to get back to work, please."

"Come on, Jo." Micky elbows me in the biceps. "Take it in jest and just go over to her. Get your bloody books signed already."

I look to Kristin for support, or perhaps, for a clear sign that it's okay for me to do so. She's the boss, after all. "This is beginning to sound like workplace harassment," I say, when Kristin remains silent as she's wont to do.

Kristin takes a step in my direction and puts her hands

on my shoulders. "Trust me. You'll make Caitlin's day. She's not all that famous here in good old Oz. She must be getting attention-starved by now. You'd be doing *her* a favor."

I glance over at Caitlin and see her looking over at us. What must the three of us look like whispering like this behind the counter?

"Fine." It is why I put the books in my bag in the first place. Why they've been in there for days—days without me mustering up the courage to approach her. And now my boss has given me permission. "Just don't stare at me like I'm an attraction in the zoo."

"We have work to do," Micky says, shooting me a wink.

"I'm expecting Sheryl back any minute, so you'd better hurry," Kristin says.

"Okay." I fetch my bag in the back, take a deep breath, and walk over to Caitlin James, my feminist heroine.

"Sorry to disturb you, Miss James." I can't keep the shake out of my voice.

"*Miss* James?" The lift of her eyebrow makes something coil tightly in my belly.

"I'm s-sorry," I stammer. "I'm a big fan of yours and you've been coming here for a while now and Kristin said it would be okay if I asked you to sign a couple of your books that I own and have read many, many times, if I may add." I'm blabbering like a two-year old who's just discovered the sound of her own voice.

"Why don't you sit down?" Her big brown eyes sparkle up at me.

"Er, yes." My hands have forgotten the required motion to pull a chair back and my body—huge and looming over Caitlin—doesn't want to obey.

"It's Josephine, right?" Caitlin says, snapping me out of my daze. "Lovely name."

I pull myself together and sit down. "Thank you." Micky and Kristin's teasing has drained the confidence I need to ask Caitlin James for her autograph, let alone sit with her and have a conversation. Part of me wishes Sheryl would arrive before I make an even greater fool of myself.

"Which books do you have?" Caitlin puts her elbows on the table and leans close enough so that I can smell her perfume. Something earthy and sensual.

I pull my bag onto my lap and reach for the three books that, dramatic as it may sound, changed my life. I display them on the table.

"Well thumbed I see." Caitlin's lips draw into a smile. She takes one of the books and leafs through it. "And you love using a highlighter." She looks back at me. "There's more to you than the girl who makes excellent flat whites, isn't there?"

"I study with Sheryl. I mean, Professor Johnson. I'm one of her graduate teaching assistants and she got me this job because a PhD doesn't exactly pay the rent in Sydney these days."

"Good for you." She drops the book and intertwines her fingers. "You're in good hands with Sheryl."

"She's been very nice to me."

"She must have picked you for a reason." Caitlin opens the cover of one of the books. "Do you have a pen, Josephine?"

"Oh, er, yes." I dig in my bag, my fingers frantically feeling for the pen I put in there with the books. "Here you go."

I try to watch as Caitlin signs three of her books that I've owned for almost ten years, but it's hard to keep my gaze trained on her. It feels like too much of an intrusion. She holds the pen gracefully and is scribbling away when I sense a presence behind me.

"Am I interrupting?" Sheryl asks.

I nearly jump out of my skin. Sheryl puts a hand on my shoulder. She knows all about my admiration for Caitlin James, yet in all the time I worked for her, she never mentioned that she and Caitlin go way back. I only found out when Caitlin returned from the United States and walked into the Pink Bean one day.

"Just signing some books for Josephine." Caitlin sounds merry.

"I'll leave you to it then." Sheryl turns to me. "Could you stay behind for a bit after your shift? I'd like to discuss Naisha Turner with you. We can have lunch, if you like."

"Sure." I can't say no to Sheryl, though I don't have the spare cash to go out for lunch. As usual, because Sheryl knows about my sister, she'll offer to pay, but I have too much pride to let her.

"Come upstairs when you're done," she says, as though she can read the anguish right off my face. "I'll rustle something up."

I nod and heave a small sigh of relief as she heads over to the counter and slings an arm around Kristin's waist.

"She really does take good care of you." Caitlin leans over the table conspiratorially. "But if you ever need any gossip on Professor Johnson, I've known her since she was an eighteen-year-old tomboy," she jokes.

This is one of those moments in which I wish so very much I was the sort of girl who has the confidence to say something clever back, but not even on my best days—and certainly not when I'm sitting opposite Caitlin James—am I skilled at coming up with witty repartee.

Caitlin goes back to signing the books in silence.

"All done." She hands me back the pen. "Thank you for reading my books." She looks me straight in the eye. Another round of blushing starts at the base of my neck. "It was an honor to sign them for you." She leans against the back of her chair. "What's your thesis on? Anything I can help with?"

Oh no. I will happily discuss my thesis subject with anyone but Caitlin James. "Body positivity among different gender identities and sexual orientations."

She nods. "Interesting."

My cheeks feel like two scorching balls of fire.

"Maybe you can tell me all about it some day." She must have sensed the discomfort of a girl clearly at odds with her own body researching body positivity. "I'll let you get back to work before I have Kristin on my case."

"Thank you so very much, Miss James," I manage to mumble.

"Please, call me Caitlin." She gives me a wide smile.

I don't need a mirror to know my face is the color of a very ripe tomato.

CHAPTER TWO

It is a long afternoon at the university library. I can usually block out all the whispers and rustle of paper, but thoughts of the newly-signed books in my bag steal my concentration and focus. When I arrive home, I find my roommate Eva slouched all over her boyfriend Declan on the sofa. They must have heard me come in, but my pending presence obviously didn't bother them enough to stop them from having their hands all over each other. A sight I've gotten used to over the past few months.

"I made pasta," Eva says. "The kind you like."

"Thanks." The thought of food wakes up my stomach and it starts to growl.

Declan moves out from under Eva. "Do you want some wine?" he asks. "It's not too bad."

"There's an offer I can't refuse." I shrug off my coat and force myself to sit with them for a bit. I was the one who used to sit in the three-seat sofa with Eva and watch the mindless reality TV shows she likes so much. But ever since things with Declan turned more serious, the atmosphere in our small flat has changed. Adding a man to the mix will do that. I have nothing against Declan, who is doing his PhD in Computer Science and is an even bigger nerd than I am, but I would like to sit in what I used to consider *my spot* on the sofa once in a while, that's all.

Tonight, however, I don't care too much. "Guess who signed my Caitlin James books today?" I can't keep the glee out of my voice.

"No way." Eva sits up. "You asked her?"

"Asked who what?" Declan gets up and fetches me a glass.

"Caitlin James."

"Jo has only idolized her for… hm, let me think, the past decade?" Eva says.

"I've never heard of her," he says.

I suddenly like Declan a little less. I reach into my bag to present him with the evidence of Caitlin's greatness.

"Is she like a modern day Germaine Greer or something?" he asks after inspecting them.

Bless his heart for trying. "More like the Australian Gloria Steinem," Eva says.

"I don't know who she is either."

Eva shakes her head and play-pushes him away. "All that time spent in front of a computer and having a girlfriend who's getting a doctorate in Gender Studies, and it never occurred to you to google feminism?"

Declan widens his eyes. "I—I don't…" he begins to say.

Now I feel sorry for the poor sod. "Caitlin has been teaching in the US for more than ten years, and wrote a couple of very well-received books along the way. And now she's back in the country," I say.

"And happens to be one of Professor Johnson's oldest friends," Eva adds and takes the book from Declan's hands. "Did she write anything special?"

It almost feels like sacrilege to watch her flip the cover of my well-worn book and read what Caitlin wrote in it—for me.

"To Josephine, who makes the best flat whites," Eva reads out loud.

I huff out a giggle. "I guess she was out of inspiration by the third one." I hold the other two books protectively against my chest.

"Come on, Jo. Let me see, please." Eva reaches out her hands.

"Oh, go on then." I'm too proud of my prizes not to share them with my best friend.

"To Josephine, the girl with the most beautiful first name," Eva reads. "That one's a bit better, I guess."

"To Josephine, may you achieve great things. That's my favorite," Eva says. "Did you get to talk to her?"

"A little." I recall that morning's stunted conversation and cringe-worthy exit with a strange kind of fondness. The illusion of the infatuated, I guess. It doesn't matter how much of a fool I made of myself—and knowing myself, it could have been much worse—I got to talk to her and I have her autograph, etched in the pages of those books forever. It would help if I didn't have to serve her coffee nearly every morning, but that too can be seen as a great gift. I'll just have to practice my deep breathing and elevate my sense of self-worth.

I give Eva and Declan the highlights of meeting Caitlin, then retreat to my room with a half-full glass of wine and a plate of the pasta Eva made. I eat too much of it while watching a documentary on my laptop. Today, I don't care about mindful eating and recognizing signs of fullness in my stomach before I overeat.

When I wake up the next morning, I reach for my phone in what has become a reflex. Before I'm even fully awake, I press the first number in my favorites. Bea will be waiting for my call already.

"Hello, Beatrice speaking," she says, her words official but her voice chirpy as ever.

"Hey, Bea. It's me." Hearing her voice always puts a smile on my face. "Did you sleep well?"

"I woke up twice," she says. "Once to go pee and the other time because Andy next door was shouting. He yelled something about a fireman. I thought there was a fire."

"Did someone come in and comfort you?"

"Yes. Nurse Annie. She's nice."

"Good. What are you doing today?"

"It's Friday so Mommy and Daddy are coming to visit."

"That's great. Will you say hello to them from me?" I always ask; Bea always forgets.

"Yes, and I will also tell them that you called and that you're doing great." She goes on in her high-pitched, carefree voice. "Have a nice day, Josephine," my sister says earnestly just before she hangs up.

I don't get up immediately but search for the last picture of the two of us together, taken two Christmases ago at her boarding school. We're both wearing Santa hats and pulling faces and she looks so happy and unperturbed. I smile because I can't help myself. My younger sister has had that effect on me since the day she was born, even though it was clear that she was different. I sometimes wish I had her straightforward and uncomplicated outlook on life.

———

The first thing I do after I get out of bed is put on my running gear. Fully dressed, I head into the kitchen and pour myself a large glass of water to wash down my morning supplements with. While I'm swallowing, I download the latest episode of the *Mindful Eating* podcast to my phone. Then I'm ready to go.

Running makes me feel more free than anything else, which is why I do it every single day. I go out first thing to avoid the pitiful glances I can't seem to get used to. *Look at that big girl trying to run*, they seem to say. Even though I've been running long enough to build up a respectable speed, I will never be the most light-footed of joggers. I often see runners who appear to be floating on thin air, their footfalls so light, they're almost flying.

Another side-effect of being too aware of people noticing me, is that I run too fast—even for my trained lungs. It happens without me noticing, until it's too late, and

I'm so out of breath—heart pounding, eyes watering—I barely make it home. Yet another reason to run before most of the city gets up. It helps that I live near the university and most students are late risers.

I blast up the volume of the podcast and start with a light jog. I only discovered this podcast a few weeks ago and have been working my way through the backlist, as I've done with most subjects that are even remotely about food, eating habits and the futility of going on a diet.

The presenter's voice is so familiar to me by now, it's comforting. Though, today, I find it hard to focus on what she has to say. She's going on about Oprah and the amount of shares she bought in Weight Watchers and what could be the reasoning behind it. A topic that would normally interest me, but my mind keeps skittering away.

Caitlin usually arrives at the Pink Bean around eleven and stays until lunch, drinking an astounding number of flat whites.

"In Boston, they've never even heard of it. I tried to have them make it for me, but it's just not the same as a good old Aussie one," I heard her say to Kristin once.

Up until yesterday, I'd barely had a conversation with her apart from exchanging the usual pleasantries that come with serving someone coffee. What could I possibly have to say to Caitlin James?

I turn a corner and focus my attention back on the podcast. At first, I tried running without any entertainment in my ears, but the heavy sound of my feet on the sidewalk was too confronting. Then I tried listening to music, but I found myself singing along, quite loudly as it turned out, and decided I couldn't deal with the strange looks I got from the people I ran past. Then I discovered podcasts and found out I could be learning and running at the same time. It's been a match made in heaven ever since.

The presenter appears very disappointed with Oprah for backing Weight Watchers, a company whose business model is based on people perpetually regaining weight, driving them back to the scales and the points system. How else can they make money? Like most big girls, I've done my time with Weight Watchers. I lost a few pounds, but nothing significant. Like most women, I've tried every diet under the sun. I'm an academic. I do research for a living. If all goes well, I'll be able to put Doctor of Philosophy on my business card in a few years. I consider myself one of the smart ones, yet every diet I used to read about gave me enough hope to try it. None of them has ever worked for more than a few months.

A man I see every morning with his Labrador running on a leash beside him nods as he passes. I can't help myself. Not even the endorphins my body is producing at this very moment can keep me from wondering what he must think of me. Which leads me back to wondering what Caitlin must think of me. She was very courteous—of course she was. Any other woman so surrounded by out lesbians and aware of Caitlin's reputation would have attempted to flirt with her, but not me. Girls my size don't flirt. We do the opposite. We hide ourselves away behind silence and awkwardness. Behind blistering low self-esteem because everywhere we look we see the message loud and clear: what is wrong with you for being this size?

I run a little faster—try to outrun the thoughts in my mind. Sometimes it works, which is one of the greatest pleasures of running. It makes me forget who I am for half an hour a day. Maybe I should start listening to feminist podcasts again instead of all this mindful eating crap.

When I've run my route and stand panting, hands on knees, in front of the door of our building, one of our neighbors comes out. He knows me so doesn't need to give me a once-over, doesn't need to do a double take at seeing the fat girl come home all sweaty after a run—at the incongruence of it all.

"Good on ya," he says, and walks away.

CHAPTER THREE

"Wet cap, please," Robin says, as she does every day. She's on her way back from CrossFit and just stopping by to give Micky a quick kiss.

"One latte coming right up," I joke.

Robin winks at me as we go through our daily ritual, then heads over to where Micky and Amber are sitting—next to Caitlin's regular table, which is still empty.

Amber gets up as she sees Robin approach and throws her arms wide. I see a lot of these women, catch quite a few bits and bobs of their drama, but I'm an outsider. The young one. Sheryl's student. Kristin's charity case. I don't belong in their group, which is fine with me—I'm not looking to socialize with my bosses after hours. What my outsider status does, however, is give me a unique chance to observe them. Micky's drama with Robin before they got together. How their relationship is quickly evolving now. Kristin and Sheryl's ups and downs. That time they all returned from an open AA meeting in support of Sheryl—no one told me, but I'm not stupid—which was also the very first time I saw Caitlin in the Pink Bean.

And today: the return of Amber. She's been gone for a couple of months. Micky's been beside herself with excitement for days.

Amber talks and Robin listens. Micky looks around. She has probably heard Amber's big Indian yoga retreat story already. Our gazes cross and she quirks up her eyebrows. My gut tells me Micky won't be working at the Pink Bean for much longer. Of all the people Kristin has employed, I've been here the longest. Maybe because I need the money the most.

"I gotta run," Robin says. "We'll catch up tonight."

Amber waves at me and points at her cup. I brew her another cup of tea and bring it over.

"How are you doing, Josephine?" she asks. "I didn't get a chance to ask earlier."

"I'm fine, thanks. Welcome back. We've missed you."

"You don't say." Micky taps her fingers against Amber's hand. "We have so much to catch up on. It's all well and good to go away for a while, but you can never again go to a place where they only allow you internet access once a week."

Amber rolls her eyes. "Always one to exaggerate, you."

I stand around, watching them. Ever since I started working here, which wasn't very long after the Pink Bean opened, these two have been coming here.

"Sit with us for a bit," Micky says. "The boss is away and there's no one here."

"If only Kristin knew." I pull up a chair.

"Today is special." Micky beams. "Amber is back."

I nod.

"We've been having many special days around here," Micky continues. "Josephine met her idol Caitlin James yesterday."

Now it's my turn to roll my eyes, even though the memory of sitting at a table with Caitlin only twenty-four hours ago washes warmly through me.

Amber almost chokes on her tea. "Caitlin James?"

"Oh. That's right. I had forgotten about that," Micky says. She leans back with her eyes crinkled into a smile.

"Forgotten about what?" I sit up a bit straighter.

"Amber knows Caitlin very well."

My palms start sweating. I don't know why.

"That woman." Amber shakes her head. "She's a predator."

"She is?"

"I had a one-night stand with her," Amber says matter-of-factly.

"Don't mind her, Jo. Amber is still upset that Caitlin didn't want to continue their short-lived affair."

"That's absolutely not true. In hindsight, I'm glad nothing came of it."

"What happened?" I wouldn't normally be so forward, but I'm dying to find out.

"I'm not one to sleep with another woman just like that. But Caitlin came after me hard that night and I was in bed with her before I knew what her deal was. No monogamy, blah, blah, blah. Going back to the States in a few days, blah, blah, blah. She was only back in Sydney for the opening of the Pink Bean. She wasn't upfront about her intentions and I don't like that at all."

"Sounds to me you're more upset about you not sticking to your principles for once—and getting laid in a spectacular fashion, because of it, by the way—than about Caitlin leading you on a bit," Micky says.

My pulse has picked up speed. So much inside information on Caitlin just falling into my lap. Although a pang of jealousy makes its way through my mind. Amber slept with Caitlin. And told Micky it was spectacular. It figures that Caitlin would go for the gorgeous likes of Amber. The thought of them together sends a shiver up my spine.

"No, Micky. You know what I value most in any relationship, no matter how brief or fleeting, is honesty and being genuine. What Caitlin did was lure me into bed under false pretenses."

"It's so good to have you back, Amber." Micky shakes her head, a big smile on her face.

The door opens. We all look up.

It's Caitlin.

She looks around until her gaze rests on our table. She narrows her eyes. "Amber? Is that you?"

"Here we go for the charade," Amber mutters under her breath.

I don't know where to look or what to do first. Caitlin is walking toward us, and I want to see her greet Amber after what I've just heard, but I also want to be ready behind the counter when she orders her drink.

"I heard you were on some Hindu retreat?" Caitlin says as she reaches us. She puts her hands on the sides of Amber's arms and kisses her on each cheek, as if they're old friends. I guess they are in a way. The two of them together. I can't chase the image from my mind. They would make a stunning couple.

"Yoga," Amber says dryly.

"That's right. How could I forget?" Caitlin takes a step back. "How have you been? Can I join you?" She doesn't wait for a reply, just pulls up a chair and sits down.

Only then does Caitlin spot me. She just says, "A flat white, please." That's it. I've rarely felt less significant. As usual, nobody notices. I'm the invisible one with the huge body—a contradiction if there ever was one. I try to look at Micky but she's too enthralled by what's happening in front of her.

I slink off and prepare Caitlin's coffee.

———

After Amber has left, Caitlin walks over to the counter. She patiently waits in the line that has formed, doesn't order anything, but says, "Do you have time for a chat later? I've been thinking about your thesis."

"Er, yes, of course. My shift finishes at noon."

"I'll be patiently waiting over there." She grabs a bottle of free tap water and heads back to the table she was sitting at with Amber earlier.

"What's your thesis about again?" Micky, who has

overheard the conversation, asks.

"Body positivity," I reply. No matter how passionate I am about the subject, I can't get excited about discussing it with Caitlin. Maybe I do have a crush on her.

"You should talk to Amber. I'm sure she has a thing or two to say on the subject."

"Amber?" I hand the next customer his Americano. He taps his Visa card against the PayWave machine and turns around, leaving Micky and me alone. "Have you had a good look at Amber?"

"We're basically sisters, so yes, I have." Micky brings her hands to her sides.

"I'm sure Amber has her heart in the right place, but I don't expect her to understand my plight."

"What *is* your plight, if I may ask?"

"Not my plight as such," I back-pedal with a sigh. "Put me next to Amber and ask yourself which one of us has it the hardest."

"So your thesis is about you?"

"No, it's not. It's about how women like me are made to feel by the likes of Amber." Everything is coming out all wrong again. The way I'm defending my work to Micky of all people, you would never guess I've had almost ten years of university education. I can't help myself. When people like Micky—gorgeous and happy, no matter how late she came out of the closet—talk to me about body positivity, it hits a nerve. Every time. Because, looking how she does, how can she possibly ever understand what it's like?

"Amber may surprise you. She teaches quite a few larger women in her classes."

"How very nice of her." Thank goodness a customer walks in. I take the woman's order and Micky silently prepares it.

"I'm sorry if I said something wrong," Micky says when it's just us behind the counter again.

"Bad day," I say, because it's so much easier to shrug it

off than to try to explain—really explain. Especially crammed behind the counter of a coffee shop.

"Jo, I mean it. I'm sorry." She puts a hand on my back. "I've been wanting to ask. I'm having a dinner party tomorrow evening to welcome Amber back. Do you want to come? I might invite Caitlin as well."

This throws me more than any comment she's made before. Micky and I might be colleagues, but I'm not part of the group of friends she forms with Amber, Kristin, Sheryl and Martha. And now Caitlin. How can I possibly refuse this offer if she's going to be there?

"That sounds great." If she hadn't mentioned Caitlin, I probably would have said no.

"Wonderful. I'll go invite Caitlin right now."

───────

"You've really been thinking about my thesis?" I ask, my voice already wavering. I'm getting tired of my schoolgirl crush on Caitlin. I could be getting valuable information from her. This conversation could really move things forward for me, even though my thesis is a long way from finished. But how I feel when I sit across from her is holding me back.

"I'm not one to let an interesting topic slide. You haven't made it easy for yourself by going down that route." She gives me a smile. "Besides, I have a little time on my hands these days." She pushes her chair back and makes to get up. "You want to come back to my place? I live just down the road."

My eyes go wide. I quickly push myself up, but not without shoving the side of my ass clumsily against the table, and making the cups and saucers on it tremble with a loud clang. "Sure." My voice sounds as uptight as I feel. But hell yes, I want to see where Caitlin lives. Never mind that I have survey questions to prepare this afternoon. This is much more important.

CHAPTER FOUR

"I didn't know feminism was so lucrative." I let my gaze wander around Caitlin's penthouse apartment again. My eyes can't seem to get enough of it.

"Feminism isn't, but television is," she says casually.

I'm drawn to the wall-length bookshelves opposite me. I also like the space of Caitlin's apartment. A place where I can move uninhibitedly.

"I have something for you." Caitlin catches up with me and peruses one of the shelves. "She was a brilliant student of mine and seeing as you like autographed books so much." Caitlin hands me *Your Body is Not Your Being* by Ursula Attwell, the poster child of the fat acceptance movement in North America.

"For me?" I take the book from her and automatically flip back the cover to reveal the inscription on the title page.

To Professor James, to whom I owe everything, it says.

"It's dedicated to you. I can't accept that."

"You really don't want it? Or are you just being polite?"

I chuckle. Strangely, I can deal with this kind of forwardness better than with any banter. "Okay then. I'll gladly accept." Eva will go mental over this.

"Good." Her voice sounds as if she wouldn't have taken no for an answer either way. "Micky said you're going to that dinner at hers tomorrow as well."

"Yes." This is turning out to be the strangest of days. First, Micky's invitation. Now, standing here with Caitlin in her apartment talking about it. Whatever will I do with myself tomorrow? I might have to run a marathon before I can ring Micky's bell.

"Do you know if Amber is seeing someone? I take it she isn't, what with her being away for so long." As she talks, Caitlin leads me to the couch facing her library. Her apartment is certainly grand, but she has managed to make it look warm rather than showy.

We sit, and I say, "No, she's single, though I know Professor Waltz is very interested in her."

"Professor Waltz as in Martha, Sheryl's friend?" Caitlin sucks the air out of her cheeks. "Really." She keeps her gaze pinned on me. "You must know a lot about them as a group."

I cock my head. "I really don't. Only what I pick up from working at the Pink Bean."

"Well, yes. That's what I mean. The silent bystanders are always the ones who know most." She folds her lips into a smile. "It's not easy, you know. Just coming back to Australia like that. Part of me feels like a coward for leaving the States now, when the country needs voices like mine the most. But the last election truly gutted me. And I'd been toying with the idea of coming back. I never saw myself staying in the US and growing old there. It's just not the place for it. But when you go away for more than ten years, people have moved on. Most of the people I was friends with before don't even live in Sydney anymore, apart from Sheryl." She gives a small shake of the head. "We were such good pals back in the day. The kind that can always just pick up where we left off. She's the reason I moved to this neighborhood." She suddenly scoots up. "How rude of me. I haven't even offered you anything to drink. Please, allow me to serve you this time."

I smile up at her. "Just some water, please?"

"Water? Are you kidding? I know we have to keep our urges in check around Sheryl, but come on, let's have something stronger."

"Just the one then. I'm driving."

"We'll get you an Uber if things get out of hand." Caitlin opens what looks like an authentic seventies sideboard to reveal an extensive booze collection.

Uber. She must be kidding. The only reason I even have a credit card, with the tiniest credit limit I could get, is for extreme emergencies. Getting home after a bender isn't one. Besides, it's Friday afternoon. Caitlin might be on a sabbatical, but I most certainly am not.

As she pours amber liquid into a glass, I push the amount of work I have to the back of my brain. Having the job at the Pink Bean is a godsend, but it does eat into my time. I take a deep breath and think of this as necessary research, though I know very well I'm only fooling myself. This is a pure fan girl moment. I allow myself to enjoy it, and relax my hunched-up shoulders a little.

Caitlin hands me a glass and her eyes linger on mine for a split second. I promptly forget all about my other work.

"When did you get back from the US?" I vow to push my insecurities aside and enjoy the moment. For someone with as many hang-ups as I have, that means having a normal conversation. I'm also curious. I want to know everything about Caitlin James that her Wikipedia page doesn't mention.

"Just a few weeks ago. I got lucky with this place. It had been on the market for a while and it came with some furniture I actually like."

"It's really nice." I let my gaze wander around again. I think of my and Eva's dingy flat, now often even more unkempt because of Declan being there half the time. He probably spends more hours there than I do.

"So, body positivity, huh," Caitlin says after a sip of her drink. I haven't tasted it yet but the bitter smell of whiskey wafts up my nose and makes me feel queasy. I haven't had lunch yet. "It's a big movement in the States, but not so much yet here, to my knowledge. If you need introductions to anyone in the US for an interview, I can help."

"That's very nice of you." I bring my lips to the edge of the glass and tip it back gently. The liquor stings my throat and makes me cough. Caitlin doesn't seem to have the same problem. She sits there all cool and casual, one long leg slung over the other, leaning back in the sofa as though she's about to be photographed for the back of one of her books.

"I was in your shoes a long time ago, so I'm happy to help. Though back in the days when Sheryl and I were PhD students, body positivity wasn't much of a subject yet, let alone part of a movement."

"Different times have different things to fight for." I put the glass down because the smell is starting to make me sick.

"Are you? Fighting for something, I mean?"

"Aren't all of us in the Gender Studies department? We're a small group, but we all have strong beliefs." I think of the long talks, deep into the night, Eva and I used to have before Declan came onto the scene.

Caitlin gives a small smile. "Do you know what I did my thesis on?" She slants her head back a little, exposing a pale neck. "God, it seems so long ago."

"Of course I do. Polyamory and non-monogamy in a historical and religious context."

"Have you read it?" Her eyes are back on me.

"I've read most of the dissertations written for the Gender Studies department in the past twenty years."

"Good grief. That's dedication."

I tilt my head sideways. "I think it's normal."

Caitlin scrunches her lips together and nods. "You're a serious one. I like that." A hint of a smile again. "Have you thought about what you're going to do once you have your fancy degree that no corporation will take seriously?" She holds up her hands. "Hey, I should know."

"It would be great to teach." Of course, I've thought

about it, but options are limited. If only I'd had the common sense to get an MBA. I'd most likely have a high-paying job in a bank somewhere by now; and my parents and I would never have to worry about having enough money for Bea's care. But I followed my heart when I decided what to study. I'd rather work in the Pink Bean four hours a day and follow my passion than worry about other people's money all day long.

"It's not all it's cracked up to be." Caitlin shifts in her seat, drinks more whiskey. "It used to be, but over the years, it all has become much more politicized. Grant money has gotten tighter. People in general—even the students—have become much more uptight."

I wonder if I'm included in Caitlin's definition of *uptight people in general*. "It's early days for me. I have at least three more years to go."

Caitlin nods. "Enjoy them. I never realized it then, but those years before I got my PhD were magical."

"Do I detect some nostalgia in your tone?"

"Maybe." She circles a fingertip over the rim of her glass. "I wonder if that's the true reason I invited you here. It's like a glimpse into my past."

"Have you thought about what you're going to do now you're back in the motherland?"

"Give me a break. I've only just returned home." She chuckles and the sound of it loosens something in me. I reach for my glass of whiskey. "I might write another book and do some guest lectures. Sheryl and I have been talking about me doing one at Sydney Uni. Who knows, maybe I'll even be allowed on television if ever a women's issue comes up."

"So basically do here what you've been doing in the States?"

She juts out her bottom lip. "Yeah. We're all creatures of habit, after all."

This makes me think of my own habits—and how I'm

breaking them today. Mornings are for earning money. Afternoons for research and all the tasks that come with being a Teaching Assistant. It has been like that for two years now. Drinking whiskey in a beautiful, interesting woman's penthouse in the middle of the day is very much not part of my routine. Teaching the graveyard tutorial on Gender and Media on Friday afternoons at three, however, is. I'll need to have some lunch before I teach and stop by home. Traffic will be hell to get to Camperdown. I don't want to—I'd like to sit here and chat with Caitlin all afternoon—but I need to get going.

"Thank you very much for inviting me into your home." I push myself out of the sofa, trying to do it as elegantly as possible. "I'm teaching this afternoon so I need to get a move on."

"Of course." Caitlin rises in one fluent, graceful motion. "You're always welcome here." She puts her glass down and walks me to the door. "Don't forget your book."

I stand by the front door awkwardly, unsure of how to appropriately thank her for the gift.

"I'll see you tomorrow at Micky's." Caitlin brings her hands to my shoulders, touching them lightly, and pecks me on both cheeks.

CHAPTER FIVE

When I work at the Pink Bean, I usually wear jeans and a T-shirt. I can't possibly show up at Micky's wearing what is essentially my work uniform. I wonder what Caitlin's outfit will be. Will she glam it up? There's no doubt in my mind about what Sheryl will be wearing. The same clothes she always does: faded jeans, button-down shirt and if she's feeling frivolous, a vest.

I've been invited to Kristin and Sheryl's for dinner before, but that was entirely different to tonight's event. I'm of half a mind to ask Declan if I can borrow his bike so I can have a drink and relax a little more, but it's a half hour journey to Darlinghurst and I don't want to arrive all sweaty.

I heave a sigh. I feel like a child going to a grown-up's party.

"Can I go as your date?" Eva asked me this morning. "I'm so jealous."

"Are you jealous of my nerves as well?"

"Relax. It's going to be great."

"Micky only invited me because she felt sorry for me. And I don't have anything to wear."

"Why so negative?" Eva's voice was stern. "Caitlin will be there, remember?" Eva could hardly offer me a swanky item from her wardrobe to borrow.

"How could I possibly forget?" Ever since asking her to sign those books, Caitlin has occupied most of my thoughts.

I pull the black and white polka dot dress from its hanger. I bought it at a thrift store for twenty dollars three years ago. It's the most festive piece of clothing I own so it will have to do. I tie a black bow into my hair, apply some lipstick and head out of the door to Micky's.

———

When I ring the bell, Amber opens the door, reminding me again of how close friends they are.

"It's always the ones who have to travel the farthest who arrive first. I really appreciate that, Josephine," she says, and kisses me on both cheeks.

I hand her the cheap bottle of wine I've brought, hoping she'll dispose of it discreetly before anyone sees it. It's one of the reasons I arrived so early I had to sit in my car for ten minutes before ringing the bell.

"It smells really good in here." I follow Amber into the open plan living room.

"Micky is currently wrestling with a mushroom risotto —"

"I'm done fighting." Wearing an apron, Micky comes to greet me. "And for your information, it would have been a seafood risotto if someone were not vegan."

"And I believed you were happy to have me back," Amber says.

Micky kisses me on the cheeks, ignoring Amber.

"Lovely place," I say, hoping Amber will hide the wine soon.

"About time I invited you after all the time we've spent behind that counter together."

"I have taught you many a barista secret. That's true."

Amber is rummaging around in the kitchen and, to my relief, the bottle of wine is out of sight before the bell rings again.

"I'll get it," Amber shouts.

While she's opening the door, Micky says, "She won't say it as such, but she's a little overexcited about seeing

Martha again."

"Ah." I sit and think about Caitlin questioning Amber's relationship status yesterday. I'm glad Professor Waltz is coming tonight.

Martha, Robin, Kristin and Sheryl arrive and there's a flurry of activity and pecks on the cheeks.

"Hi, Josephine," Martha says. "Don't you live near uni? If I'd known you were coming, we could have hitched a ride together." It makes me wonder who else doesn't know I was coming.

We all sit. Amber pours drinks, wine for most, apart from herself and Sheryl.

"Of course, Caitlin is late," Sheryl says.

"Look who's talking," Kristin replies. "The number of hours of my life I've spent waiting for the two of you."

"But we're worth the wait, aren't we?" Sheryl, dressed exactly as I had predicted, pats Kristin on the knee.

By the time Caitlin arrives, I've finished my first glass of wine, and I make a mental note to take it easy. Sheryl might be the most casual person, but she's still my boss. I don't want to make a fool of myself in front of any of these women.

"Don't you look nice," Caitlin says, causing my cheeks to catch fire instantly, after kissing me hello. She ends up sitting next to me in the sofa and I try not to let my thigh bump into hers too much.

"I know we're not here to talk shop." Sheryl turns herself toward the corner of the sofa where Caitlin and I are sitting. "But I've managed to convince Caitlin to do a guest lecture next week. Josephine, if you would be so kind as to make Professor James feel as welcome as possible. Give her the VIP treatment."

"Is there any other?" I turn to Caitlin. "You're in good hands with me."

"Oh, I know." She gives me an unsettling wink, then turns to Sheryl. "We've been getting to know each other better." Her tone is so suggestive, my breath catches in my throat.

"I'm in charge of entrees." Amber gets up.

"I'll give you a hand." Martha follows her into the kitchen.

"Good to know the chemistry between those two is still through the roof," Kristin says.

"True, but Amber is still Amber. So…" Micky's tone is musing.

"We can hear you," Amber shouts from the kitchen. She and Martha burst out into a giggle.

———

When we sit down to eat, everyone seems to organically pair up, especially Amber and Martha, and I'm left sitting next to Caitlin. I've had two glasses of wine, the second one sipped slowly, and the mere thought of sitting next to her in such a configuration does something to my stomach. Which is good, because then I won't eat too much. Not that I ever would in company.

"Looks like you're stuck with me," I say to Caitlin.

"I wouldn't call it stuck." She gives me the widest smile I've seen on her. Something else shoots through me. Asking me up to her place yesterday. The offer to help with my thesis. The compliments she keeps paying me tonight. No. I push the thought away. It's not possible. She's just playing. Perhaps even testing me. Or trying to make Amber jealous, not that she would notice in a million years.

A self-conscious stiffness descends on my limbs. I reach for my freshly refilled glass slowly in order not to knock anything over on the table.

"A toast to Amber." Sheryl raises her glass. "Good to have you back."

"This means you have to go back to yoga," Robin says to Micky. "No more laziness for you."

"I really believed you were practicing for yourself these days and not just to do me a favor," Amber says, a scolding note in her voice.

"I tried to get her to try CrossFit, but to no avail." Robin giggles.

"I don't have a death wish, thank you very much," Micky says.

"But you *do* like getting your hands all over your girlfriend's CrossFitting abs," Robin jokes.

"I shan't even try to deny that."

"I'll go with you, Micky," Sheryl says. "Now that I'm sober I seem to have so much extra time on my hands."

For a while, Sheryl was pretty out of it at work. I'd always known she liked a drink—who doesn't?—but things got pretty ugly for a couple of months. I'm in awe of how she has sorted herself out.

"Maybe we should all go," Caitlin butts in.

"I'll give you a private group lesson. You can pay by becoming loyal members of the studio I plan to open soon," Amber says.

I tune out the conversation, because I don't want to listen to their plans for communal exercise. There's no way I will ever share a yoga studio with these seven living and breathing ads for fitness after forty, let alone squeeze myself into a locker room with them. I'll work out the way I've been doing for the past ten years: alone. My ample breasts strapped into a bra that looks more like a piece of armor, which is probably the most expensive piece of clothing I own. Keeping my breasts in check while I run is one of the only luxuries I afford myself.

I pray the conversation will flow toward the topic of Amber's studio, something I've heard mention of in the Pink Bean for a while. Her trip to India must have galvanized her plans. But Sheryl especially seems very keen on the idea of private yoga sessions for their group. Kristin encourages her, while Martha grumbles and Robin says she's not a yoga person.

"We don't all have to go," Robin says. "I for one think

it's most important to do the kind of exercise I love. It shouldn't be a chore."

"Oh, this should be good." Micky leans back and crosses her arms over her chest.

"I'm not biting," Amber says. "Robin is right. With yoga in particular it's very important to come to the mat with the right intention. I'm not saying a challenge amongst friends isn't as good a starting point as any, but I wouldn't want anyone to feel forced."

"Let's think about," Caitlin says. "No need to make any decisions right now."

Sitting so close to me, I wonder if she can sense how uncomfortable the conversation is making me.

"Your very own studio, heh?" I ask Amber. If no one else will steer the topic that way, I gladly will.

"All I need is a bunch of money and a suitable space," she says, on a sigh. "Piece of cake."

"You can do a crowdfunding campaign," Robin says.

"Or talk to some bankers I know," Micky adds.

"We should talk," Sheryl says. "Not only do I have more time on my hands, our wine budget has shrunk as well." She gives a self-conscious chuckle.

I excuse myself to go to the bathroom while they continue their conversation about yoga. I check myself in the mirror and try to imagine what Caitlin saw when she said I looked nice. I squint, tilt my head, smile broadly, but for the life of me, I can't see it.

CHAPTER SIX

Sunday is the only day of the week I don't go for a run, but I get up early all the same because I have to call Bea. I tried negotiating with her to call at a later time, but she wouldn't budge. After I've spoken to her, I try to get back to sleep, but the dinner party rummages around in my mind.

Martha and I ended up taking a taxi together—she doesn't do Uber either, though I suspect for different reasons than me—and my car is still in Darlinghurst. I need it to get to the Pink Bean in the morning so I have no choice but to pick it up sometime today.

No matter how much work I have to catch up on, Sunday is my day of hibernation and complete relaxation. I'd much rather work a little harder during the week and have one complete day to myself than start doing little things on Sunday. Because little things always lead to bigger things and before I know it, I'll be working seven days a week.

Before Declan, Eva and I used to have Netflix marathons or go see a movie or just hang out and catch up. These days, however, Eva's Sundays, as well as most evenings, are reserved for her boyfriend. It's not that I don't understand—of course I do—but still, it stings to have become the fifth wheel in the place where I live.

At least I managed to subtly convey that for a couple of hours every Sunday, I would like the place to myself.

Not for the first time since waking up, my thoughts drift back to Caitlin's hug goodbye last night. As much as I want to believe it, I can't. She's probably got a date lined up with some goddess this very afternoon. Still, it was nice to be the recipient of that kind of attention. It has been a while. My last relationship ended more than a year ago and, just like Amber, I'm decidedly not a one-night stand girl.

I see how students look at Sheryl sometimes, who at almost fifty—and if you like the type—is still a striking woman. A lot of students seem to like the type very much. My type, not so much. When Sheryl hired me as her TA she gave me some advice on how to politely decline the inevitable invitations from students. I've never had to put her advice to use.

I roll onto my back and listen for sounds in the flat. Nothing. Officially meeting Caitlin James and all the subsequent thoughts I've had about her have had a certain, not to be misunderstood effect on me. I slide a hand inside my panties and spread my legs. I imagine that the hug good-bye she gave me last night—pressing her chest hard against mine—happened the day before, at her place with no one else around. I remember the long finger she circled the whiskey glass with and imagine that finger plunging deep into my underwear right now. Her lips trailing from my cheeks to my neck and back up to my mouth. Caitlin's lips kissing me and her finger drawing insistent circles around my clitoris. "Don't you look nice," she says, again, with an appreciative nod of the head.

It's all I need. My finger moves fast and meticulously. My thoughts do the rest. I come hard while thinking of Caitlin. I can't wait to see her tomorrow. Will she have something nice to say to me again when she comes in for her coffee?

———

To clear my head, I decide to walk all the way to Darlinghurst to pick up my car. It's a nice enough day.

Even though it's shorts and T-shirt weather, I slip into my good old pair of jeans anyway. For all the books I read on wearing whatever you want no matter the amount of cellulite on your thighs, putting it into practice does not come easy. That goes for most books I read on the topic of my thesis. It's all well and good to see it in black and white, to absorb the theory and be buoyed by uplifting words for a few hours, but changing how I've felt about myself for as long as I can remember takes more than reaching the end of a few books, obsessively following the right kind of blogs, and endlessly trawling through Tumblr for body-positive images.

It doesn't take an experienced psychologist to guess why I picked the topic for my thesis. When I talked to Sheryl about it for the first time, she was enthusiastic and as supportive as a mentor can be, but I could see that glint in her eyes. That slant of understanding in the way she held her chin. Whether imagined or not, for me, the condescension was there. It has always been there.

But it's Sunday and I don't want to think about my thesis, which is hard to do because I'm reminded of it every time I catch a glimpse of myself in the reflection of a shop window. As though, despite having been this size all my adult life, it still shocks me every time I catch myself off guard.

No informative podcasts today, only music. I put on the only playlist I've made recently. It's called *Women*, partly because I lack imagination and partly because it only consists of Adele, Sia, Lady Gaga, Whitney Houston and Christina Aguilera songs. I wish I wasn't walking down the street, so I could sing along from the top of my lungs instead of just mouthing the words.

When we both still lived at home, Bea asked me to sing her to sleep every evening. "Your voice is so beautiful, Jojo," she used to say, with the kind of admiration in her words only children can muster.

When "Alive" by Sia comes on, I glance around me. The nearest people are far enough away for me to belt out a few notes without them hearing.

"With a voice like that, it's a crime to not sing in front of an audience," Eva said after we'd just moved in together and she heard me sing in the shower.

"Never," I told her, without giving her any further explanation. Maybe if the stage was blacked out and the audience lit up so they couldn't see me. As much as I love to sing, the jubilant, alive and care-free emotions it ignites in me would be undone instantly with a spotlight on me.

A car pulls up to the curb next to me. I don't stop singing because this is the really good part of the song, but the car keeps pace with me. I pause and take a look. This is a No Stopping zone. Who does this person think they are? Whatever they think they're doing is illegal *and* rude.

I see Caitlin smiling at me. The window slides down and she leans over the passenger seat.

"I thought that was you," she says.

I pull the headphones from my ears and just stare at her. My brow is sweaty, my cheeks surely flushed an unhealthy red. Did she hear me sing?

"Need a lift?" she asks when I persevere in my stunned silence.

"I'm picking up my car. It's just around the corner," I stammer.

"I'd like to ask you something. Hop in?"

I open the car door and slide in next to her, because, really, when Caitlin says something like that, I'm not just going to keep on walking. I slam the door shut. Images from earlier this morning—from the fantasy I conjured up—flash through my mind.

"How are you?" she asks.

That's what she wanted to ask me? It doesn't matter. I'm too elated to be embarrassed by the sweat trickling down the back of my neck and my stunted breathing.

"I'm good. You?" I look at her. She has her eyes on the road.

"Ten years of driving in the US has left me a little

insecure about driving on the left side of the road." Her tone is serious. "Hang on. We're almost there."

We sit in silence. I wrap my headphones cord around my phone and stash it in my purse while hoping my walk in the sun hasn't made me sweat so much she can smell it in the confined space of her car.

"Which one is it?" she asks as we drive into Micky's street.

"That battered blue thing over there." I point at my twelve-year-old Honda.

"Very vintage." A smile in Caitlin's voice.

"I wish. Just old and rusty."

She stops next to my car and turns to me. "Would you like to go out some time?" she asks.

I furrow my eyebrows. Did my ears get damaged earlier because I played Sia too loudly? "Sorry? What?"

"Can I take you out to dinner some time this week?"

My brain is about to short-circuit. My mouth knows what to do, apparently. "Yes. Of course. Er, that, er, would be—"

"Great." She beams a smile at me. "We'll set it up tomorrow when I come in for my coffee."

"Sounds good." The sweat that has trickled all the way down my spine pools in the small of my back. "See you then." In order for me to process this, I need to get out of Caitlin's car as soon as possible.

"I look forward to it."

"Thanks for the ride." I stand there trembling in my sneakers while I watch her drive off. Did this just actually happen? I look around as though wanting to find some physical evidence. There is none, of course. Only the warm, exhilarating memory in my mind of Caitlin asking me out.

In the evening, it's just me and Eva. The perfect opportunity to tell her about Caitlin asking me out, but I don't. She'll only freak out, which would freak me out even more.

Besides, if I tell her, I'll have to go through with it. Part of me already knows I won't be able to. I haven't fully reached my conclusion yet, because I so wish I was the kind of person who could go on a date with Caitlin James. But I'm the opposite. And it's not even because I'm fat and she's a gorgeous, brilliant, well-spoken feminist. Not too much, anyway. It's about all the other shit I carry around with me every single moment of every single day. It's about the absolute certainty that I *will* make a fool of myself. I'm already smitten with her, already don't really know how to carry myself around her.

Aside from that, I'm convinced—utterly, truly certain —that she has only asked me out because of some silly bet she has with someone. Sheryl would never be so cruel, but maybe some of the others who were at the dinner party are. It's not as if it's never happened to me before.

Then there's the ominous reason my previous two relationships ended, which is a silly reason to even think about in the context of a first date with Caitlin—as if we would ever get to the point of doing *that*. The whole idea of us going on a date is ludicrous. My brain simply cannot compute. Besides, I'll have to work with her when she comes to the university to give a guest lecture. I'd rather do that knowing I bowed out gracefully instead of giving in to the lunacy of getting to know Caitlin better over a nice meal and a bottle of wine.

Still, there's a small part of me that wants to shove all my doubts and fears to the side and just go. Just live. Just feel like a normal person for once. But that part, no matter how much it bursts with desire, will never win. I've always been much more a head-over-heart kind of girl. I never had much choice.

"You're awfully quiet," Eva says. "What's going on?"

"Nothing. Where's Declan?"

"At his place."

"Oh, I didn't even know he still had a place of his

own." I don't mean to snap at her. Although it does bother me that Declan spends so much time at our place, under normal circumstances, I would never address the topic in this way.

"Come on." Eva pauses whatever is playing on TV. I was so caught up in my thoughts I don't even know what we're watching. She pulls her legs under her body and turns to me. "What's going on?"

"I'm sorry. I shouldn't have said that. Declan is a great bloke. I'm happy for you guys, you know that."

"I know he's been spending a lot of time here. If you'd seen where he lives, you'd understand. The place is a tip."

"I'm sure it is."

"But that's no excuse. I just ushered him in here, into *our* home. We can have rules, if you want to. Or certain days he's not here. Girls' nights for us."

"I guess I miss you," I blurt out. Anything to not have to talk about what I'm really struggling with.

"I miss you too." A pause. "Things have been moving so fast with me and Declan."

"Maybe one more night a week where it's just the two of us would be nice."

Eva nods. "You got it. How about Wednesdays?"

"Sure." I look at Eva from under my lashes. The way she and Declan are together, I can see the writing on the wall. Eva and I can try to make a last-ditch effort to spend more time together as roommates, but he has wormed his way not only into our home, but into her heart as well.

"Sundays and Wednesday are exclusively ours from now on." She cocks her head, gives me a stare. "Are you sure there's nothing else you want to talk about?"

I've already given her the low-down on last night's dinner. I shake my head. "Thanks, but I'm fine." As I lean my back against the sofa, I realize I use that lie too often.

CHAPTER SEVEN

Micky has come down with the flu, so it's just me and Kristin at the Pink Bean the next morning. I've gotten so used to working with Micky, it takes me a while to readjust to having Kristin so close by. She's usually around, but not this hands-on—unless things get really hectic. Though the vibe is different because she's the boss, I don't mind because I'm sure Micky would have given me the third degree about sitting next to Caitlin at hers on Saturday and a whole load of other nonsense. Kristin is much more business-like.

"I'm swinging by Micky's to check in on her. But no caffeine for her today," Amber says when she comes in for her daily green tea. "Give me two cups of tea, please."

"Wish her well from me." A short conversation with Amber is all I have time for that morning, until the queue shortens and it's just a few regulars scattered around the shop nursing cups of coffee. I was glad it was busy because now that things have quieted down, every time the door opens, or someone so much as shifts a little noisily in their seat, my heart flings itself against my chest.

How is rejecting Caitlin better than not going on a date with her? I ask myself during a bathroom break. But over the years I've gotten used to biting many a bullet like this and I prefer a minute of pain over an outstretched period any day of the week.

When she finally comes in, a little later than usual, she's dressed in a tight pair of jeans, a satin blouse with a flowery pattern loosely hanging from her frame, and a pair of heels so high her feet must hurt.

Kristin and I don't have the silent agreement that I always serve Caitlin, so while I stand around awkwardly, she says, "Looking very glamorous today, *Miss James*."

"I have a meeting with a publisher. Might as well spruce up a bit for the occasion." When she sees me, she smiles. It's a different smile than any of the ones she's shown me before. Like she's really happy to see me. *Me.*

Kristin asks her a few questions, but I'm too mesmerized by the red of her lipstick to pay attention to the conversation they're having. The way her neck is exposed because she has pinned her dark hair up into a complicated twist is not helping. My body and mind are screaming at me to make this agony end. I need to talk to Caitlin.

Once she has settled at her table, I ask Kristin if it's okay to take a little break. Whereas Micky would have surely given me a suggestive wiggle of the eyebrows, Kristin just says, "Of course."

"Hey." Again, I'm flummoxed by Caitlin's appearance. Because of the mascara she has applied, her wide brown eyes look even bigger than usual today. "Can we talk for a minute?"

I would give a lot to not have to do this at the Pink Bean, but at least Micky is not watching my every move.

"Of course. Please sit."

I take my seat, my hands drop down in my lap and I look at my fidgeting fingers because I don't know where else to look. But this is Josephine Greenwood in survival mode. It's sad that I've been here many times before, avoiding disasters before giving them a chance to happen.

"I'm very flattered that you asked me out, but, er, it's not going to work out for me."

Caitlin leans back, pushes her chair back a little so she can sling one leg over the other. "I'm not sure I know what you mean."

"I can't go out with you. I'm sorry."

"Why not if I may ask?" She sounds as though she's actually interested, not as if she has already won a bet with herself. *How long before Josephine loses her nerve?*

"It's, er, difficult to explain." I throw a glance at her but avert my eyes immediately. "It's just… it's not right."

"You say you want to be a teacher. Why don't you try explaining regardless of how difficult it is?" There's a sudden sharpness to her voice.

"You must have looked in the mirror this morning. Now you're looking at me. Something clearly doesn't add up."

"What the hell are you going on about?"

Fat. Ugly. Poor. The words repeat in my head like the polar opposite of a positivity-inspiring mantra.

"I'm absolutely certain that in Darlinghurst alone there are a dozen women who would love to go out with you. As for me, I just can't do it."

"Well." The word comes out at a short, wounded snap. "I'm not going to beg for it."

"I'm sorry. It's not you. I think you are amazing, but I just… can't."

"Whatever you say, Josephine." At least I don't hear pity in her words. I don't hear any sign of understanding either. But it's better this way.

"I'm sorry," I mumble again as I get up. I don't look back. On the way to the bathroom I try to take a few deep breaths, but I can't even do that. Fists balled, I stand in the stall for long agonizing minutes.

CHAPTER EIGHT

"Everything set?" Sheryl asks.

"Yep." It's the day of Caitlin's lecture at the university. Four miserable days after I told her I couldn't go out with her. I can't help but wonder if she told Sheryl about it. If she has, Sheryl hasn't said anything.

"I just spoke to Caitlin on the phone. She should be here in half an hour." Sheryl takes off her spectacles and squints at me. "Are you okay?"

"Must have caught the tail end of Micky's flu," I lie. None of my symptoms are physical.

"Do I need to order you on bed rest?"

I heave a big sigh. "I think it would be better if Mona played welcoming committee to Caitlin."

"If you feel unwell, please go home, Josephine."

"It's not..." The words get stuck in my throat again, as they always do.

Sheryl scrunches her lips together. "Wait a minute. Has Caitlin been up to her usual tricks?" That pout again. "Did something happen between the two of you?" She holds up her hands. "Tell me if it's none of my business, but she should know better than to mess with my teaching assistants."

"No, no, it's nothing like that. It's my fault. I handled it all wrong. I mean, I didn't want to..."

"What's going on? You're unraveling in front of me," Sheryl says.

Oh, what the hell. I need to talk to someone about this. Sheryl might not be the ideal choice, what with her being my boss and Caitlin's friend, but she's also an open-minded, intelligent and strong woman, whom I've known for a long time.

I close her office door behind me and sit in the visitor chair unbidden.

"She asked me out. I said yes. Then I realized I couldn't possibly go out with her, and said no. She's hardly said a word to me at the Pink Bean since, which I get. But having to welcome her here is so awkward. I'm sorry to let you down because of something so stupid."

"Why did you change your mind about going out with her?" Sheryl drums her fingertips on her desk.

"Because… I shouldn't have said yes in the first place, she just caught me off guard. And she's Caitlin James. Of course my gut instinct was to say yes. But can you imagine her and me on a date?" I shake my head. "The thought is ludicrous."

"Why?" There's genuine surprise in Sheryl's voice.

"Because she is Caitlin James and I am me."

"I'm used to much better arguments from you."

"It doesn't make sense. I can't for the life of me figure out why she would even ask me out."

"Maybe because she likes you?"

"What? No." I shake my head to emphasize my beliefs.

"Why is that so impossible for you to fathom?" Sheryl gives an incredulous huff.

"It's just not possible."

Sheryl draws up her eyebrows. "Well, I say it's perfectly plausible." Sheryl's tone is insistent. "And I've known Caitlin for a very long time."

"You really think so?" Sheryl wouldn't make something like that up. "Because I find it very hard to believe she would genuinely be interested in someone like me."

"Oh, Josephine." Sheryl looks at her watch. "I wish we

had more time for this conversation." She shakes her head. "I will tell you this, though. A while back Caitlin asked me for some names of experts on body positivity. I told her that despite your relatively low profile, Caitlin could do a lot worse than to approach you."

"You did?" I'm surprised, but feel too uneasy because of having put Sheryl in a position where she feels she has to cheer me up to have her words sink in properly.

"Of course, but if I'd known you felt this way about yourself, Josephine... Most students who have come as far as you have don't. All the things we discuss in lectures and tutorials... But I guess real life is more complicated than that."

I'm having trouble keeping up with Sheryl's train of thought.

"Let me tell you one more thing." She puts her spectacles back on and leans over her desk, regarding me intently. "You are just as worthy to go on a date with Caitlin as any other woman she has ever asked out." She scoffs, probably remembering Caitlin's reputation. "And there is absolutely nothing wrong with you and her going out. Nothing." She pauses. "Well, she is quite a bit older than you, but that's not the issue at hand here, I believe."

I so desperately want to believe Sheryl's words, but she doesn't know what it's like. She hasn't walked in my shoes— she can't possibly fathom how much my feet, and all the rest of me, suffer under the weight of my body.

"Thank you for saying that." I get up. "She's about to arrive. I'd better welcome her."

"Okay. Josephine, I always mean what I say." Sheryl pushes her chair back. "Let me just put my vest on and I'll go with you."

———

There must be three hundred students attending Caitlin's lecture, many from departments other than ours. The auditorium is filled to the brim and at the back there are double rows of people wanting to catch a glimpse of her.

On the podium, she shines. She talks with an ease I admire and perhaps also envy a little. I've watched numerous YouTube videos of her but it's different when you're in the same room. The energy she projects and the charisma that drips off her have the audience enthralled.

I try to attentively listen, drink in every word she says about the differences between feminism in the United States and Australia, how in some fields we are years behind and in others we've just naturally taken a huge lead. But seeing her up there is distracting, even for an academic like me. During the ten minutes Sheryl and I spent with her before the lecture she gave me the cold shoulder again. For someone who thrives on making herself as invisible as possible—oh, the irony—it stung. Having her attention taken away from me does not feel like a relief at all.

I look at her, at her confident hand gestures and the way she can get the crowd to break out into laughter on cue, I realize I might have made a mistake. No matter what Sheryl or anyone else says, I'm still convinced Caitlin and I shouldn't go on a date—the incongruence of it is too much for my mind—but I should have handled it better when I said no. I never believed Caitlin could have felt rejected by the likes of me.

I'll need to talk to her again. Ask her out for a drink. Maybe some sort of friendship can be salvaged from the mess I've made of this. Because she's too much to ignore, to just forget about. Seeing her nearly every day at the Pink Bean isn't helping—and it's not as if she'll suddenly start frequenting another coffee shop. I need to make this right, somehow.

The audience breaks out into a loud cheer. I missed the end of Caitlin's lecture. But these are modern times and guest lectures like this one get recorded and the video distributed online. I'll be able to watch it over and over again.

I get up from my seat in the front and position myself against the wall, waiting for the auditorium to empty.

"That was amazing." Eva sidles up to me. "Can you introduce me?"

"I'm not sure." I can just about suppress a groan.

"Oh, come on. I thought you were thick as thieves now?"

"Some other time, okay? Look at her. The woman is being bombarded." I nod at the front of the room where Caitlin is being surrounded by a mob of enthusiastic students. Good thing I'm not on bouncer duty.

"Yeah, don't really want to mingle with those first-year groupies. So beneath me," Eva says. "I'll take a rain check."

"I don't remember giving you one." I shoot her a grin.

"I know you'll come through for me either way, buddy." She winks. "See you later."

I watch Eva walk off and wait patiently for the crowd to thin. It takes forever and Sheryl finally steps in. As the group of people disperses, Caitlin appears in my field of vision again, and something coils in my stomach. Can I ever truly be friends with her without constantly pining for more? Provided she would even want to still be friends after the way I treated her.

"Will you escort Caitlin to wherever she wants to go please, Josephine? I'll catch up with you later. I just got a message from the Dean." She rolls her eyes. "He wants a debrief. Now. Tsk."

"I still know my way around this place, you know," Caitlin says. "I was only a student here for about ten years."

"That may be so, but we can't have you wandering around here all alone. Not for yours or the students' sakes." Sheryl elbows Caitlin in the arm gently. "Gotta go. Why don't we meet at The Flying Pig later?"

"Do you have an office here?" Caitlin asks me, her voice flat.

"Yes."

"Can I use it for a couple of minutes just to decompress?"

"Of course." We walk to my office. Though the turn-out for Caitlin's lecture was big, the campus is quiet because it's Friday afternoon.

What I call *my office* is a glorified broom closet, filled to the brim with books and papers. There's really no room for two people in there.

"I'll give you some space." If I had known Caitlin was going to be in my office, I would have made it look a lot more acceptable. Just before I close the door behind me, I turn around. Caitlin's looking around, her eyes flicking left to right, her presence making the room feel even smaller than it is. "Can we talk for a second? I'm really sorry about the other day. I didn't mean to make you feel…" Feel what? *Christ.* I should have prepared this little speech better, though I know that no matter how many times I practiced the words in advance, they would never come out the way I would want them to.

"Can I sit in your chair?" she asks.

"Sure." I lean awkwardly against the door frame.

"Close the door, please." It's uncanny how it already feels more like her office—her turf—than mine.

I close the door and lean against it.

"I'm listening," she says, making me feel like I'm taking an oral exam I haven't studied for at all.

"I went about it all wrong. I hope you didn't even for a minute feel it was about you or, er, that it was a rejection of some sort, because it wasn't."

"I agree that you handled it wrong. And please explain how I'm not supposed to perceive it as a rejection when it so clearly was?"

"Because…" I hate having to stand up like this, towering over her—over the entire room. "I wasn't rejecting *you*. I was rejecting myself as someone suitable to go out with you."

"And how is that different exactly?"

"You know I'm a fan of yours. I've admired you for years. Surely you must know it's not about you."

Caitlin shakes her head. "Those are two very different things. It's not because you're a fan of my work that you'd want to go out with me. I've admired many a person in the course of my life, but I've rarely wanted to take them out for a drink. Well, at least the kind of drink I wanted to take you out for."

"I'm not good enough," I blurt out. Oh shit. I bite my bottom lip, hoping it will stave off tears.

"Says who?" Her eyes flick over me.

"Says me," I stammer.

"And who made you the judge of that?"

Pull yourself together now, I say to myself. I take a deep breath and respond to her glance. "How about we go for a drink and try to be friends?"

"Friends, huh?" Caitlin pushes herself out of my chair. "We can try." Something playful crosses her face. "I've always liked a challenge."

————

"I'm not usually drawn to such lack of confidence," Caitlin says. We're sitting in The Flying Pig, waiting for Sheryl, who has already texted me to say she'll be a while. "But I guess it took some nerve to say what you just said. In its own way."

I'm not sure what to reply to that. "I'm sorry," I say, again, feeling foolish.

"You must stop apologizing for who you are, Josephine. I'm surprised that wasn't the very first thing Sheryl ever taught you."

"Perhaps it was, but I might have forgotten." I give her a small smile. "My first class with Sheryl was quite some time ago."

"Were you immediately smitten with her?" Caitlin's drawing circles around the rim of her glass again.

I puff a breath through my nose. "No, though she was

very impressive."

"She's been through a lot. I'm not even sure this is a good place for us to meet, even though she's the one who suggested it." A quick raise of her eyebrows. "Oh damn, did I just say too much?"

I shake my head. "I know she's a recovering alcoholic. It's kind of hard not to when you're her TA."

"Phew." Caitlin draws her lips into a smirk. "I sometimes have a tendency to speak before thinking."

"Not today in that lecture, though. You were amazing."

Caitlin perks up—something she always seems to do when I give her a compliment. A subtle straightening of the spine and a little glint in her eyes. "Ah, students are easy."

"Tell me about it," I quip.

"Tell me about *you*. That's the deal I'm willing to make if you want to be friends. Until Sheryl arrives, you need to tell me some things about yourself. It's entirely up to you what you say." She sits there gloating.

I inhale deeply and take a sip from my wine. "Okay." I pause to think. "I go for a run almost every day." I search her face for any sign of surprise, but find none. She just rests her chin on an upturned palm and looks at me through hooded eyelids. "I share an apartment with my best friend Eva, who would love to meet you." I shift on the bar stool, take another sip. "The other day when you drove up to me, I was singing a Sia song very loudly. I like to sing."

Caitlin doesn't interrupt me, just stares at me intently.

"I guess one of the reasons I was so reluctant to actually go out with you is because Amber said you and her had, er, you know, and it made me believe that was the type you were going for."

"I don't really have a type as such," she says. "And variety is the spice of life."

I have to laugh at that. "I have heard the rumors, of course."

"Please, enlighten me." Caitlin smiles back at me.

"It is said that you're a bit of a player, I guess. Earlier, even Sheryl hinted at it. She thought I was upset because you had been up to your 'usual tricks' again."

Caitlin nods thoughtfully. "I have two things to say about that." She holds up her index finger. "The first one is a long exposé on non-monogamy, which is not what most people think it is. I won't go into detail now, because Sheryl will surely roll her eyes at me if she hears me talking about it when she arrives. But hey, we'll have plenty of time to talk about that once we're friends." A sparkle in her eyes. "Second, and more importantly because I couldn't really give a rat's ass about my so-called reputation, why were you so upset?"

I want to take another sip but find my wine glass empty. "I was enjoying getting to know you so much. It was like a dream come true, really. When you asked me out, at first I was totally taken aback and of course I said yes. But when I started thinking about it, as I tend to do, I was sure it must have been some kind of hoax. Or the result of a nasty bet. Anything that didn't have to do with you actually liking me and wanting to go out with me. I freaked out."

Caitlin sucks her bottom lip into her mouth before she speaks. It makes her look even more attractive. She has dressed to impress again today in a cream pants suit and bold, red blouse. "You know what this reminds me of? My time in grad school. My friends and I, Sheryl included, used to have conversations like this all the time. Analyzing everything to death before it even had a chance to happen." She finds my gaze with hers. "Sound familiar?"

"I guess."

"For the record, and because some people just need certain things spelled out for them: I do like you, Josephine. But if you want me to back off and if my advances make you feel uncomfortable, then I'll shut up. Simple as that."

"I—" I start saying something I haven't thought through at all when Sheryl arrives.

"Glad you two are getting along again," she says. "Another round?"

"We can go somewhere else," Caitlin is quick to say.

"Here is just fine. What are you having?"

When Sheryl heads to the bar, Caitlin leans over the table and says, "Even though I've made plenty of mistakes in my life, I have few regrets. Not being there for Sheryl when she needed me most and being too preoccupied with myself to even see something was going on with her is one of my biggest regrets. She's had it rougher than most, I'll tell you that."

"Sometimes you have to go through stuff on your own. That's the only way."

"Ain't that the truth."

Sheryl comes back with the drinks. Wine for me and Caitlin, water for herself.

"The Dean must have talked your ear off," Caitlin says.

"I think he's about to offer you a permanent position. You know, one of those prestige professorships that have more to do with image than substance." She chuckles.

"Well, thank you very much," Caitlin says. "That's so very American."

Sheryl raises her glass. "Thanks for a wonderful lecture. If we can acquire you, Gender Studies will become the most popular department."

"I'm feeling very popular right now. The other day I got approached for a position at ANBC as well. You know Zoya Das?"

"Zoya Das of the TV show with the same name?" My ears have certainly perked up.

Caitlin nods. "I met her in the States a few times and we've been friendly since. She called me up yesterday, asked me to come in for a meeting with the head of the Cultural News Division. It's all set up for next Tuesday."

"You're moving up swiftly in the world," Sheryl says. "And, oh yes, I know who Zoya Das is."

"She came out a few years ago." I'm just stating the obvious. I guess I'm trying to find out something about Caitlin's friendship with her.

"Who do you think told her to finally get over herself and do it? The amount of revenue she generates for that network. And this isn't the nineties anymore."

My eyes go wide. "You?"

Caitlin brings her arms wide and shows her palms. "I'm a woman of many talents."

"That's really great news," I say. "Good luck." I'm none the wiser about Caitlin's relationship to Zoya. All I know is that they would make a striking couple together. I make a mental note to google Zoya Das later and find out everything there is about her private life. Frankly, it would surprise me if a woman like her were single.

"How did that meeting with your publisher go?"

"Not bad," Caitlin says. "It's early days, but I may have another book in me. I pitched some ideas, though there's one I'm very enthusiastic about." She looks at me. "Body positivity and fat acceptance in Australian culture. And I think I know someone who can help me with that."

My belly tingles. I'm both elated and miffed. The conversation I'm part of astounds me—all this talk of TV shows and books—but what Caitlin just said puts all that has passed between us into a new perspective. She wants to pick my brain on my thesis subject. It's all starting to make sense.

"What do you say, Josephine?" she asks.

"I'm here if you need me." I down my glass of wine in a few big gulps.

CHAPTER NINE

The next Monday morning at the Pink Bean, Micky is alive and kicking again—and in great verbal form. Probably because she's had to shut up for the better part of a week.

"And do you know what Olivia said to that?" she asks. I haven't really been listening. The first few weeks she worked here, Micky was so shy. Now she won't shut up.

"No," I say.

"She told Christopher 'to go fuck himself'! Can you believe that? I truly thought I had raised them better than that. But kids these days have so many outside influences…" She goes on and on about video games and violence and foul language in movies. I'm relieved when Amber walks in.

When you work in a coffee shop, the regulars become sort of like extended family. Now that she's back, I certainly see much more of Amber than I do of my own family. It makes me think of what Bea asked me this morning.

"When are you coming to visit me, JoJo?"

I could almost hear her heart break when I said I didn't know, even though her birthday is coming up. I can't take my old Honda on a long road trip to Northwood and money for air fare is hard to come by after the fee for another term of Bea's boarding school has just come out of my bank account. But she doesn't know that, of course.

I see a look pass between Micky and Amber and after a beat, Amber asks me, "Can I have a minute of your time, please, Josephine?"

"Sure."

"I'll hold the fort," Micky is quick to say. "I'll bring over the drinks."

All thoughts of my sister are pushed from my mind. I'm curious to find out what they have been talking about behind my back.

"The other night at Micky's dinner," Amber starts, "you didn't really say much about all of us doing a yoga class together. I wanted to talk to you about that in private." She clears her throat. "Is it because you have a special dislike for yoga or because you think the classes are not inclusive or any other reason?"

The thing with Amber is that her entire demeanor is so open and inviting and non-threatening, she can get away with saying anything. Not that this is particularly offensive. I'm glad she asked—I've been asked much worse.

"I've never really tried yoga. I'm just not much of a group exercise person. I run. Alone."

"You're a runner?" A hint of surprise in her voice.

I nod. "Have been for a very long time."

"I have lots of runners in my class. I've been thinking about offering a yoga for runners class when—well, *if*, I guess—I ever open my own studio. Would you be interested in that?"

"I don't know. I also run because it's free. I don't have much spare cash lying around." I narrow my eyes. "Is this some kind of one-woman survey?"

Micky brings over our drinks and scurries off.

"No, no," Amber says.

"Just level with me, Amber. Ask me what it is you really want to know."

"Micky told me about your thesis subject and it made me think. The stereotypical image of yogis is people like me. Or housewives in designer gear strolling through Darlinghurst with their mat rolled up under their arm. I see it in my classes all the time. In some of them, everyone looks so alike. There's no diversity. But I want my studio to be for everyone. That includes all body types."

"That's great." What else can I possibly say?

"I'm not just trying to sell something here, Josephine. I'm nowhere near going out on my own yet. I just want to start a conversation. For me, yoga is about the absolute opposite of what kind of pants you wear when you practice it. And it's not about how far you can bend over and whether you can reach your toes or not. It's about breath." She taps her chest. "The most vital part of life. And listening to your body. That's why I wanted to talk to you. Because of what you're working on. I believe we operate in the same field."

"Well, apparently even Caitlin James is going to write a book about body positivity now. You can always consult with her."

Amber waves her hand dismissively. "I'd rather talk to you."

"You don't like her very much, do you?"

Amber sighs. "I don't know her all that well. Though I'm guessing that will soon change. Everyone here seems to think the world of her." Amber intertwines her fingers. "What do you make of her now that you've gotten to know her better?"

This question rattles me more than all the ones that have come before combined. "I—I quite like her," I stammer.

Amber nods in a way that indicates she knows exactly what I mean by that. "Be vigilant. That's all I will say about it."

"We're just friends. Nothing's going on between us," I hurry to say.

"I should probably have a conversation with her about what happened two years ago. I shouldn't let it stand between her and me getting on. She probably doesn't even know how I feel about how she treated me."

"What *did* happen back then?" If Amber can ask me

uncomfortable questions, so can I.

Amber inhales deeply, then locks her gaze on mine. "It was the opening night of the Pink Bean. I was over-excited about the fact that a couple of lesbians were opening a coffee shop between my place of work and my home. Sheryl introduced us and I might have had a bit too much champagne. The waiters just kept refilling my glass without me having much chance to notice. I had no idea how much I had actually drunk—something I usually keep vigilant track of. Caitlin pretty straightforwardly hit on me and we went home together." She finally drinks from her tea. "Things, er, happened. Fun things. I liked her. She was very outspoken and confident and unafraid to communicate in bed, you know?"

I nod, even though I don't know a thing about it.

"She stayed the night. We had a nice morning together. Then—and only then—she said she was flying back to Boston the next day." Amber shakes her head. "It's not as if we didn't have time to chat before she ended up in my bed. She willfully omitted the information to get her way. I didn't appreciate that at all."

"Did you tell her?"

"No. She was leaving anyway. In hindsight, I should have said something." Amber puts her cup down. "It's just that when it comes to meeting new people, I tend to trust my gut. I didn't see through her at all. The champagne had something to do with it as well. I'm not really one to sleep with someone just after meeting them. It doesn't really excite me. I'd much rather know the woman. I guess I was equally upset with myself for lacking judgement. Micky has been mercilessly teasing me about it ever since."

"She sure is at the tip of everyone's tongue." I can't help but smile a little when I talk about Caitlin.

Amber shrugs. "It happened two years ago. Time to move on."

"For what it's worth, I hope you'll be able to open your

studio soon. I think it's great that you're trying to be as inclusive as possible."

"I think it's important." She shifts in her seat. "Anytime you're interested in taking a free private lesson, let me know, okay? The offer will never go away."

"Thanks. Was there anything else you wanted to ask me? You and Micky seemed to be totally in cahoots about something?"

"You know Micky, she likes to make a fuss over nothing. I might pick your brain later and I would love it if you could recommend some literature on the subject of body positivity."

"I'll make you a list." I look at Amber and get the impression there are quite a few things she hasn't asked me yet.

"Aha, two people I wanted to see." Caitlin's voice booms behind me. I hadn't even noticed her coming in. "Dinner. Saturday. My place. Don't worry, I won't be cooking any of the dishes myself."

Both Amber and I look up at her. Amber speaks first. "You know I'm vegan?"

"I sure do." Caitlin gives a little bow. "Will you ask Martha for me? She doesn't hang around here that much."

"You want *me* to ask Martha?" Amber asks, vexed.

"Aren't you two seeing each other?" Caitlin's appearance is much like a bull's in a china shop.

"I'll ask her. I'll probably see her at uni later," I say, helping Amber out. Her relationship status with Martha is still very vague.

"And you, Jo. Bring a friend. Didn't your roommate want to meet me?" Caitlin says it as though it's the most normal thing in the world.

"If she can tear herself away from her boyfriend for a night." I'm sure Eva will gladly cancel any plans with Declan for an evening at Caitlin's penthouse.

"Just let me know a few days in advance."

As Caitlin walks away in Micky's direction, it strikes me that she didn't even ask Amber and me if we were free.

"She's a force of nature," Amber says. "I really can't blame myself too much for taking her home with me that night."

"I'd better get back to work. I'll think about that yoga class."

As I head behind the counter, I wonder if Amber is still a little hung up on Caitlin.

CHAPTER TEN

"Oh my god, oh my god, oh my god," Eva says. "I can't believe this." We're in the elevator to Caitlin's penthouse. Eva has come by the Pink Bean a few times and has met most of the others, but this experience is just as daunting to me as it is to her, even though I've been to Caitlin's place before. I'm glad to have my best friend by my side.

When we ring the bell and the door opens, I have to blink twice.

"Hi. Come on in. I'm Zoya." Zoya Das, barefoot and looking very much at home in Caitlin's apartment, lets us in.

"And the evening has only just started," Eva murmurs.

Zoya kisses us on the cheek as though Eva and I are old acquaintances.

"Who is it?" Caitlin yells from somewhere deep in the apartment.

"You must be Josephine and..."

"Eva."

"Ah, yes. Welcome to our soirée. Well, it's not my soirée. But I'm delighted to meet you." She leads the way through the sitting area and onto the patio. We're the first to arrive. "I'll be right back with some drinks. You both drink champagne?"

Eva and I nod like school girls asked if we want to go on a trip to the zoo.

"Jesus Christ," Eva says. "Pinch me, please. Is this real?" She puts her hands on the balustrade and takes in the view over the city. "And did Zoya Das just ask us if we drink champagne? What kind of circles do you travel in these days, Jo?"

The kind that make me feel very dumpy and unglamorous, I think. "This is all very new to me."

"Here we go, ladies." Zoya returns with an open bottle of Perrier-Jouët. Behind her, an actual waiter carries out a tray of champagne flutes. "Caitlin will be right out. She's just bossing around the chef."

I catch Eva's glance. She looks just as wide-eyed as I feel.

The waiter silently pours us a glass each.

"Let's not wait for the host. Cheers." Zoya holds up her glass. I look into her dark eyes. She's casually dressed in jeans and a sleeveless shirt and she looks absolutely beautiful. I make it my mission for the night to find out whether she and Caitlin are sleeping together. I've had ample time to google Zoya Das and all recent articles I found were about her and her long-term partner breaking up a few months ago.

The bell rings and Zoya dashes out.

"Are they—?" Eva whispers, reading my mind.

I shrug. "I don't know, but I'm sure we'll find out soon enough." I can't drink from my glass of champagne fast enough.

Amber, Martha, Micky and Robin all arrive together. As though she's been waiting to make her entrance, Caitlin only comes out onto the balcony a few minutes later.

"You've started already. Good." She kisses everyone hello.

"You must be Eva."

"Very nice to meet you, Miss James." I can't believe how composed Eva is all of a sudden. "Thank you so much for inviting me into your home."

"Any friend of Josephine's is welcome here." She shoots Eva a wink, then takes a step in my direction.

"Hey." Her voice is so low and sultry a dagger of pure

lust pierces through me. "Good to see you." She lays a hand gently on my shoulder and plants a slow kiss just below my left cheekbone.

"No need to wait for Sheryl, as usual," she announces to the group with a smile. "Cheers." Just then, the bell rings again. "I'll get it," Caitlin says.

I watch her walk inside. She's wearing thigh-hugging jeans and a black satin top which make her look like a movie star on holiday. If I weren't surrounded by a group of people, I'd ask Eva to pinch me now.

———

Of the two of us, Eva has always been the suave one, but I'm still baffled at how well she carries herself amid these women she barely knows. It must be the champagne, of which she eagerly partakes.

After drinks on the balcony, we retreat inside. To my surprise, name cards are set on the plates and I find myself sitting in between Micky and Caitlin, which is quite possibly the worst combination for my nerves. Zoya sits on the other side of Caitlin and Eva across from me.

Because I'm sitting next to Caitlin, her elbow bumps into mine occasionally which keeps igniting that arrow of lust that has lodged itself somewhere deep inside of me. But I can't see the looks that pass between her and Zoya. To figure out if they've been getting it on, I can only rely on what I hear and on what I'll ask Eva later—she has the best view. I hope she's wearing her observation lenses. By the look of things, she appears to be more bespectacled with champagne goggles.

"I love this song," Zoya says when "Breathe Me" by Sia comes on the elegantly tucked away speakers. "Now there's a fellow Australian to be proud of."

"I believe Josephine is a big fan as well. She was singing some Sia at the top of her lungs when I ran into her the other day." Caitlin looks at me and I tell myself to stop drinking immediately because it's as though I'm melting under her gaze. And to think I could have been out on a date with her. Perhaps even this very night. Why did I blow that off so clumsily and swiftly again?

"Jo is an absolutely amazing singer. I live with her. I should know," Eva says.

"Is she?" Kristin asks. "Because I've worked with her for almost two years and I had no idea." She looks at me quizzically. "All those open mics we've had, Josephine? And you never said a word?"

"Eva's exaggerating," I say.

"She doesn't sing in public," Eva is quick to add.

"You've got me all curious now," Micky chimes in. "We're having an open mic next Friday, aren't we?" she asks Kristin, then turns to me again. "You should give it a go."

I shake my head. "I'd really rather not."

"Leave her be," Amber says. "Don't force her."

"Forget about an open mic night," Eva says, "she should go on *The X Factor* or something. She'd win the whole thing without even trying."

I try to shoot her a look and make her shut up, but Eva is not intoxicated by alcohol alone. She's under the influence of the sparkling vibe of the night and it's making her ultra-chatty and forward. She's not going to shut up unless I kick her shins under the table. I try, but I can't reach them.

"You're really that good?" Caitlin looks at me. "A woman of many talents." She smiles and I feel my insides go liquid again.

"Not really," I say. "To make it very clear to everyone, I'm not going to sing next Friday. It's just not going to happen. No matter how hard you insist."

"It's your choice," Amber says. "No one else's."

"Thank you." I nod my head solemnly.

"Speaking of many talents," Zoya says. I crane my neck to see her while she speaks. "I'm this close to having this talent sign a contract with ANBC. Wouldn't her lovely face make a welcome change from all the ugly old-man mugs we seem to specialize in?" She slings an arm around Caitlin's neck. The two of them look breath-taking together.

"So you only want me for my face?" Caitlin swats her arm away, but it lingers.

"That's not very feminist," Robin says in between chuckles.

"I know. My bad. You might be too pretty for what we have in mind for you, dear Caitlin. Sorry."

"The other day," Sheryl says, "I read this article about *manxiety* and how men these days need our *fempathy*." She shakes her head. "I couldn't believe it."

"She stormed out of her study looking as if Germaine Greer had just died," Kristin says. "I was really worried for a while." She grins at Sheryl.

"Even the notion," Sheryl says, her face serious.

"Men have it so rough these days," Robin says, a touch of irony to her voice. "Look at the sector I'm in. Over the past five years, the number of females in banking has risen by one whole percent. They must be shaking in their hand-made leather shoes."

"At least there's someone else at this table who has had to deal with white male privilege on a daily basis," Zoya says. "I was beginning to think I was the only one."

"What you have done is beyond comparison," Sheryl says. "The number of girls who have grown up watching you be smart on television. A million lectures in Gender Studies couldn't have the same effect."

"If their fathers let them watch it," Caitlin says.

"Aren't we being a little harsh right now?" Micky asks.

"I agree," Martha says.

"You two only agree because you were both married to men," Sheryl says.

"Decent blokes who are excellent fathers to our children. Darren has always treated Liv and Chris exactly the same," Micky says.

Across the table, I catch Eva's glance. She quirks up her

eyebrows.

"Martha's husband left her for a younger woman. How *decent* is that?" Sheryl won't let up.

"It all worked out for the better," Martha says, her tone peace-seeking. "Look at me now?" She turns to Amber, making Amber shuffle around nervously in her chair. *Those two.*

"My boyfriend is a feminist," Eva declares.

"This begs the question: can a man ever truly be a feminist?" Caitlin asks.

The waiter comes out of the kitchen carrying a few plates. "Ready for dessert, ladies?" he asks.

"Why don't we ask him?" Eva says.

I can see the poor man's limbs stiffen. He deposits a plate with a fancy-looking dessert in front of Eva. "Carl, was it?" she asks. "Are *you* a feminist?"

Truth be told, I hadn't paid Carl much attention before. Put on the spot like that, he looks more like a boy than a man.

"Of course I am, Madam," he says. "Please enjoy your dessert."

"Good answer, Carl," Caitlin says as he goes back into the kitchen to fetch more plates. "Please don't drag the poor waiter into this," she says to Eva.

"Why not?" Eva has already tucked into her dessert even though most of the table hasn't received theirs yet. The champagne seems to be catching up with her quickly.

"I've got this." Sheryl rises and walks over to our end of the table. She puts a hand on Eva's shoulder. "Come on you, let's get some air."

Glassy-eyed, Eva looks up at her. "Really?"

"Yes." Even when heavily under the influence of alcohol, Sheryl's natural authority is not something easily disobeyed. Eva had her as a teacher for long enough to know. She follows Sheryl onto the balcony.

"I'm sorry. She's had a bit too much," I say.

"It's Carl's own fault for having such a heavy pouring hand," Caitlin says, a smile on her face.

Amid the ruckus of Carl serving dessert to the other end of the table, Caitlin leans toward to me, and asks, "How about you Josephine? Have you ever found a man feminist enough to be with?"

"Me?" I shake my head. "Even before I knew I was into girls, boys never paid me much attention." Looks like I might have had a few too many bubbles myself, otherwise I would never have said that.

"Fools," Caitlin says, stirring up something lustful inside me again.

I feel emboldened enough to contemplate asking the same question of Caitlin, but Sheryl comes back in, Eva leaning on her heavily.

"She needs to lie down a bit. Can I put her in the guest room, Caitlin?"

"Sure."

"Let me take care of her." I push my chair back and rush to Sheryl's side. Eva is my responsibility. And Sheryl is the last person who should be taking care of my intoxicated friend. I support Eva from the other side. The outside air must have knocked her out. Her head rolls onto my shoulder. Luckily, she's about a third of my size and I can easily carry her.

"Where's the guest room, please?" I ask.

"I'll show you." Caitlin gets up.

"I'm sorry again. She's such a lightweight."

I stretch Eva out onto the bed.

"It happens to the best of us," Caitlin says, and gives me a light pat on the shoulder. "I'll get her some water." She disappears into the ensuite bathroom.

"She was so excited to meet you," I say when Caitlin returns.

"Take a deep breath, Josephine." Caitlin puts the water on the nightstand, then turns to me. The room is lit only by whatever light comes in through the window. Caitlin is so close and I suddenly realize we're standing in a bedroom together, only a few inches separating us. "It's all right and it's not your fault."

"Thank you for inviting me." I want to keep her in this room with me.

"We're friends now, aren't we?" Caitlin says, slanting her head to the side, exposing her long neck.

I nod and swallow. I seem to have lost the power of speech for a moment.

"I'm glad," Caitlin says, and touches her hand against my arm again. The contact shoots through me like an electric current and jolts me out of my mesmerized state.

"I should never have—" I start to say.

"Everything okay in here?" Zoya peeks her head into the room and the moment is gone.

"Fine." I straighten my spine. "She'll just need to sleep it off." My brain goes from romantic mode into practical mode as I start wondering how the hell I'm going to get Eva home.

———

After everyone has left—including the chef, Carl, *and* Zoya —and with Eva still sleeping soundly in Caitlin's guest room, we sit on the balcony overlooking the city.

"You can catch a glimpse of the opera house if you crane your neck this way," Caitlin says.

After what happened with Eva I declined any further alcoholic beverages and I've started to sober up. The state I was in earlier, when I was about to confess to Caitlin that I should never have rebuffed her advances in the first place, seems far away. I still feel the same, increasingly so with every minute I spend in her company, but the words have long gone.

"It's beautiful."

"You can stay the night if you want to. The bed in the other room is made up."

"So many rooms in this place."

Caitlin chuckles. She's far more tipsy than I am at this point. "I know. And for what?"

"Drunken admirers who fall asleep, of course."

Caitlin tips her head in agreement. "Did you have a good time tonight?"

I nod. "It was lovely."

"I know she's going to regret it in the morning, but I'm glad your friend is out cold in my guest room. It gives us a chance to chat some more. And…" She angles her chair more in my direction. "Perhaps you can sing me a song now. Just for me. No one else."

I smile shyly. I want for Caitlin to keep looking at me the way she's looking at me now. Her eyes full of expectation and laughter. But there's no way I'm going to sing for her.

"I—I can't."

"Why? Your voice doesn't work when I'm listening?" She sinks her teeth into her bottom lip.

"Something like that." Something inside me shifts. Maybe she's only flirting with me because she's tipsy, but it doesn't matter. It feels the same to me. "Maybe some other time."

"Maybe." She shrugs.

"Can I ask you something?" This, at least, I need to know.

"Shoot." Caitlin draws her legs onto the chair and wraps her arms around her knees.

"Are you and Zoya, er, a thing?"

"Me and Zoya?" She huffs out a chuckle. "God no. Zoya is still very heart-broken about the end of her relationship. Sixteen years they were together, she and Rebecca. Can you imagine that?"

"She didn't look very heart-broken to me."

"We don't always show what we feel, do we?"

"True enough."

"Why did you ask? About me and Zoya?" Her eyes are

narrowed to slits.

"Just curious."

"Did you just want to change the subject from you singing for me?"

"I wish Eva hadn't said anything."

"Ah, Eva. Responsible for many things tonight."

"I should probably call Declan. Have him pick us up."

"Just let her sleep here. It's fine." She draws her lips into a smile. "That way you get to stay a little longer as well."

"Caitlin, I…"

"I'm sorry. Did I make you uncomfortable? I do remember I told you that I was going to back off. But Eva isn't the only one who's had a bit too much."

"I want to go out with you," I blurt out. It comes out all wrong again—not even like a question—but at least I said it.

The clatter of glass inside startles us.

"Sleeping beauty must be awake," Caitlin says.

I've already risen from my chair and am halfway inside.

"Jo? Are we still at Caitlin's house?" Eva asks. "I'm so very sorry. I broke a glass."

"Let me get that." I put Eva in a chair and scrape the shards of glass together while my mind races. I just sort of asked Caitlin out. What is she going to reply? She was flirting with me. I wasn't imagining that. I'm sure of it.

"Can we go home now?" Eva asks.

"I'll get you girls an Uber," Caitlin says and starts fidgeting with her phone. "Aren't they the best invention ever?"

We say goodbye, Eva barely able to make eye contact with Caitlin.

"I'll pay you back for the Uber on Monday," I say.

"How about you take me out on that date instead?" The bell announcing the elevator pings just as Caitlin kisses me on the cheek.

CHAPTER ELEVEN

"Did you and Eva get home okay?" Micky asks. "Or did you have to spend the night?" She smirks at me.

"We got home just fine, thank you." Although it hasn't been formally set up yet, I'm bursting with glee about my upcoming date with Caitlin. "And I asked Caitlin out."

She gives me an incredulous stare for a split second, then says, "About bloody time."

"What's that supposed to mean?"

"Oh, come on, Jo. Don't tell me you only just this weekend noticed she has been flirting her socks off with you."

"We do have a certain… rapport." I can't stop grinning.

"Chemistry, more like."

"Just don't go shouting it off the rooftops, okay? I know you and your big mouth. I'm surprised you haven't yelled it out to Kristin yet."

"I promise, my dearest Josephine. My lips are sealed. But you have to promise to give me all the details. When is this highly anticipated event taking place?"

"Not sure yet. I guess we'll set it up today."

"I'll be sure to give you lots of space when she comes in."

"Thanks." I lean against the counter and look at Micky.

"I know what you're thinking, Jo. This place has been a godsend for both our love lives."

"Let's not get too carried away. For you, yes. For me,

we'll see. How is Robin, by the way? Any news about her immigration status?"

"As long as Goodwin Stark keeps sponsoring her, she can stay. We should be good for the near future, though when you depend on a corporate institution for your partner to remain in the country, it's not the most comforting thought. She has a contract, but contracts can so easily be broken."

"I hope it works out for her. And you."

"Meanwhile, I just need to have as much hot sex with my CrossFitting girlfriend as I can."

I roll my eyes. "You've changed, you know that?"

"I don't think I've changed so much as come into my own. I was always like this, but when we first met I was too intimidated by you to reveal my true self."

"Oh, lay off, Micky."

"It's true. When I first met you I was just beginning my career as a Pink Bean barista—though barista is a big word for it because I didn't know how to work the coffee machine. Being introduced to one of Sheryl's brilliant TAs who knew how to make the perfect wet cap was very intimidating indeed. I was a divorced housewife who'd never worked a day in her life."

"And you were so very deep in the closet. It's been an honor to have witnessed your transition. Though, at times, I feel like you might have grown too confident."

Micky slaps her towel against my thigh and laughs. "You haven't even gone on a date with Caitlin yet and your arrogance has grown out of proportion already. God knows how insufferable you'll be once you've actually gone out with her."

"Not nearly as insufferable as you, I'm sure." I grin, enjoying our banter.

"I hope you'll never forget who actually gave you the courage to go up to Caitlin and get your books signed. On top of that, I did your back a big favor because you didn't have to carry around an assortment of feminist literature anymore. Don't I deserve a little bit of gratitude?"

I chuckle. The effect of love has been unmistakable on Micky. Infectious at times. At twenty-eight, I haven't been very lucky in the romance department yet. I think of the main reason my previous relationships didn't work out as expected—and one of the main contributors to my decision to cancel my previous date with Caitlin. Maybe with her—with the right person—it will be different. But I'm getting way ahead of myself.

"Does your new-found confidence mean you're going to sing on Friday?" Micky asks.

"No, of course not. One doesn't have anything to do with the other."

"Give me a break." Micky puts her hands on her hips defiantly. "I bet you a full week of cleaning the coffee machine that in less than a month's time, you'll be singing your heart out in front of all of us."

"Fine." I hold out my hand. "Let's shake on it." Though I'm certain of my case—I know myself much better than Micky does—I'm glad we're not betting actual money, only the most annoying task that comes with our job.

"Such commotion behind the counter. Please put some of that energy into my flat white." Out of nowhere, Caitlin appears in front of us. She's earlier than usual.

"Where did you come from?" Micky asks.

"Same place as every other human being, dear Michaela," Caitlin says. "I just brought some books up to Sheryl and snuck in through the back," she says to me.

"Go on. Sit down. I'll be on flat white duty today." Micky winks at me.

After we've both sat down, I give Caitlin a shy, "Hey." The new-found confidence I just displayed to Micky seems to have evaporated. Caitlin was quite tipsy last Saturday. She could have changed her mind.

"How's Eva?" she asks.

"Good as new today, I suspect. Not so good yesterday. But Declan took excellent care of her."

"Ah, to have a partner to refresh the damp washcloth on your forehead when hungover," Caitlin says. "A pleasure totally foreign to me, I must admit."

I nod, just so that I don't have to admit such small, intimate kindnesses are just as alien to me.

"Here you go, ladies. I'll leave you to it." Micky brings our beverages.

"She looks like she knows something," Caitlin says after Micky has left.

"Working in a coffee shop makes one very observant."

"You should know," Caitlin says and smiles. "Back in the day when I was a grad student, I could get by on the measly stipend offered by the university. It wasn't much, but if I was careful, it was enough. I'm sorry things have changed so much."

"Back in the day?" I cock my head.

"Does that make me sound much older than I am?"

"I love working here. I make extra by being Sheryl's TA as well. But I have more expenses than most." I quickly correct myself. "Eva seems to get by just fine." I don't want to burden Caitlin with my family situation. We'll need to go on quite a few dates before I tell her about that.

"She sure likes to gulp down other people's champagne."

"She sends her deepest apologies, by the way."

Caitlin waves it off. "Speaking of that night."

"Yes." My heart picks up speed.

"You said something rather startling," she teases.

"I understand if you've changed your mind. After all, I've changed mine twice now."

"Today's youth. So erratic." Caitlin pushes a strand of hair behind her ear.

"For the record, I'd still very much like to go out with you."

"Good." Caitlin picks up her coffee and peers at me over the rim of the cup. "When?"

"Friday?" I suggest.

"Isn't that the open mic night?"

"Yes, so?"

"I've never been to one."

"I'm not going to sing."

"I know." She takes a sip and puts her cup back down. "Can we go out on a school night?"

"I'm below thirty and you're a lady of leisure. I don't see why not."

"You've grown feistier already." She grins.

"How about Wednesday evening?"

Caitlin nods. "Sounds good. I can Uber over to your neighborhood if you like."

"You seem really smitten with Uber." I chuckle.

"I just love practical innovations like that."

"Give me your number and I'll tell you where to meet."

"You're not going to invite me for drinks at your no-doubt wonderful student accommodation first?"

This makes me think of the agreement Eva and I made about making Wednesday nights girls' nights at our apartment. I figure she won't mind—and she owes me for making a fool of herself at Caitlin's place.

"I couldn't possibly. Not after having been invited to your swanky digs."

"Don't fret, Josephine. I was just like you once. I lived in the same neighborhood and had the same job."

"That might be true, yet I think your post-grad life was very different from mine."

"Sheryl and I were around your age when she fell in love with Kristin. We didn't live together like you and Eva, but we spent most of our free time together, planning to overthrow the patriarchy." She leans back in her seat. "It was an adjustment when her relationship with Kristin suddenly became more important than our friendship." Caitlin looks up, her gaze trailing behind me.

"My ears are ringing." I easily recognize Sheryl's voice.

"I was just telling Josephine about how as soon as true love came along, you left your best friend without a wing woman at the many parties we attended back then." She turns to me. "You don't seem to party nearly as much as we did back in the day."

"What Caitlin calls a party," Sheryl pulls up chair, "were mostly meetings of the university's Lesbian Association, which, admittedly, frequently got out of hand."

"Still," Caitlin says, a warm smile on her face.

I wonder if Eva and I will still be friends like this in twenty years' time.

"I'm glad I caught you, Caitlin. Guess who just called me?"

"Hm. The Prime Minister? He has finally come to his senses and wants to consult you on the virtue of same-sex marriage?"

Sheryl sighs. "Don't you sometimes wonder how someone like Caitlin ended up earning all that feminist glory in the States? You can never get a straight answer out of her."

"Only when there are cameras around," Caitlin says.

"The Dean would like to set up a meeting with you. I gave him your number. You should expect a call any minute."

As if by magic, a ringing noise comes from Caitlin's purse.

"I'd best get back to work." It makes me feel like such a slacker when Sheryl comes down and I'm sitting around chatting.

"Can you get me an espresso, please, Jo?" Sheryl asks.

"The very picture of cougar paradise," Micky says. "You must be beside yourself, Josephine."

I give her a look and ignore her comment. Martha has

just joined Caitlin and Sheryl at their table.

"Amber should be pleased when she comes in later." I scan Micky's face. "How are things progressing with her and Martha?"

Micky shrugs. "Amber is an open book about everything, except her love life."

"But everyone can see that something's going on between them."

"If you want information, you're better off asking Martha. Or Amber herself. Who knows, maybe she'll open up to you?"

"It's just strange for me to see her in this context. Up until a few years ago Martha was married to the Vice-Chancellor. Now she's sitting here in the coffee shop where I work, chatting with her peers, one of whom I'm about to go on a date with."

"Life is strange like that."

"Earlier, Caitlin was talking about when she was my age. It sort of felt like looking into a crystal ball. Trying to guess at my future."

"The age difference doesn't bother you?" Micky is not catching on to my philosophical vibe and her question pulls me right out of it.

"Not really."

"Have you had liaisons with older women before?" Her curious streak rears its head again.

"Never." I look at Sheryl, Caitlin and Martha huddled around the round table. I might have dreamed of it, but never as much as since I met Caitlin James in the flesh. I don't voice that last thought. It would only give Micky more fodder for derisive comments.

"You mean you never lusted after me?" Micky asks. "That really hurts my feelings, Josephine."

"What has gotten into you today?"

"Not sure," Micky says, an unexpected earnest note in her voice. "Robin's away the entire week. It made me think about whether it makes sense for us to live in separate homes."

"You want her to move in with you?"

"I've been thinking about it. But I would need to talk to the kids first. They're at mine as of Wednesday. I thought I'd talk to them then."

"Big step."

"I love her. It doesn't feel like a big step at all. More like the next logical one."

A group of customers comes in and Micky and I snap to attention. After we've taken care of them, Amber arrives. She spots Martha and gives her a shy wave.

"Micky," she hisses under her breath.

"Amber?" Micky replies.

"Why didn't you text me to say Martha was here?"

Micky grins. "As per our non-existing worthy-of-teenage-girls agreement, you mean?"

"A heads-up would have been nice."

"What difference would it have made? You always look so fresh-faced and healthy. What warm-blooded professor could resist that?"

While I head toward a table to clean it off, I realize that nerves are part and parcel of any potential romantic situation. If even a woman like Amber, who spent a couple of months meditating in India, can still get so nervous about unexpectedly running into the object of her affection, then it's only normal that, already, my nerves for Wednesday are starting to mount. The reasons for cancelling the date the first time still sit somewhere in the back of my mind, mocking me. Ready to strike as soon as I let my guard down.

After I've put the dirty mugs in the dishwasher, I look up and find Micky still behind the counter, instead of on her break talking to Amber.

"Apparently, Martha is more interesting to chat to today than me." She has a smirk on her face. "Which is a definite step in the right direction in the tortured romance of Amber and Martha."

CHAPTER TWELVE

"I don't have anything to wear." I gaze into my wardrobe, not wanting to turn around and face Eva, who is sitting on my bed.

"Come on, Jo. You see her every day when you're in a Pink Bean apron. It doesn't matter what you wear."

"Of course it does. Attire states intention."

"What *are* your intentions?" Eva's chuckle makes me turn around. I scan my bed for something soft to throw at her, but come up empty-handed.

She must be surprised by the look on my face because her expression changes to one of worry. She pats the spot next to her. "Come on. Time for a best friend pep talk."

Reluctantly, I sit, the mattress inclining to my side of the bed.

"We both know you're going to wear your polka dot dress," Eva says. "This isn't about clothes so much as about your nerves acting up. And I get it. I'd be nervous too. Hell, I made a complete fool of myself in her penthouse. Rock bottom has already been reached. No matter what you wear, you will come across as mature and wise compared to me." She bumps her shoulder against mine. "Do you want to talk?"

"That feeling of dread is back. With a vengeance. Who am I to go on a date with Caitlin James? I'm not good enough. Look at me. I'm the poor fat girl who serves her coffee every day. I should know my place."

"This isn't the Middle Ages anymore, Jo."

"Sometimes I wish it were. At least women with my body type were revered back then."

"And abused, belittled and treated like mere ovens to bake children in." Eva puts a hand on my knee. "You're completely misidentifying again. You are a brilliant scholar. An amazing friend. The kindest sister and most generous daughter."

"I might be smart, but that's not what people see when they look at me. All they see is fat, which automatically translates into lazy and unhealthy in their minds."

"And you know the thoughts of all the people, do you? I wish I had that amazing ability. I would be able to tell what Declan is thinking all the time. Actually, no; I don't want to know that sometimes he wants to play video games more than be with me." Eva gets up and squats in front of me. "She asked you out, remember? You've spent a lot of time together since, and she's still raring to go out with you. Doesn't that say enough?"

"It's because I was totally fan-girling over her. I was stroking her ego."

"Please get up." Eva holds out a hand.

I take it and let her pull me up. She closes my wardrobe doors so we face the mirror that the exterior is made of. I'm still wearing the robe I threw on when I exited the shower.

"I'm going to tell you what I see when I look into this mirror," Eva says. "I see my friend Josephine Greenwood, of course, but I'll tell you what I saw when we first met, before we were friends. Not for one single second did I think of you as lazy or unhealthy. How could I? Do you know how many kilometers I run every morning, Jo? Zero. I mean, sometimes I run a few when snoozing and when I wake up it kind of feels real for a minute. And lazy? Give me a break. Laziness does not get you a teaching assistant gig with Professor Johnson. She's the pickiest in the department. You are not only smart, Jo. You work every morning in a coffee shop so your sister can go to that school. You don't have to do that. And when I read your master's thesis, I was so bloody jealous."

I find her eyes in the reflection of the mirror.

She nods. "I was. I could never put anything so eloquently as you did. My guess is Caitlin might be compulsively attracted to your brainiac capacities."

"Because she wants to pick my brain on body positivity. That's probably the main reason she wants to go out with me."

"So what if it is? It won't be the only reason, I can assure you that. Speaking of body positivity. We are both products of the same university department. We don't conform to the beauty standard imposed on us by photoshopped pictures in silly magazines. And you know who else went to that uni and studied the same subject? Hell, she even made a career out of it."

"Okay. Okay. I get it. I'll leave your money for the flattery on the nightstand."

"Would I ever be friends with the person you believe you are right now? No. I know who you are. My bet is Caitlin has caught a glimpse of it."

"Thanks, Eva." I shake my head. "I—I just…"

"Nu-huh." She curls an arm around my shoulder. "I don't want to hear it. You're writing your damn dissertation on body positivity. You live and breathe the subject. Time to act like it. You are beautiful and worthy and perfect just the way you are. I know that, deep down, you know this too."

"Have you ever considered a career in motivational speaking?" I shoot Eva a grin. "You'd be pretty good at it. You swear a bit much, but sometimes that's the only way Aussies can get their point across."

"Yeah, yeah. Come on, put on your dress and your lipstick and be on your way. If you keep stalling like this, you'll be late and you don't want to keep Caitlin waiting."

"God no. I want to be there at least fifteen minutes in

advance."

"Please tell her again how sorry I am for my behavior the other night." Eva pulls the corners of her mouth down. "I'm not sure how I can ever face her again."

"Now who's being overly dramatic?"

"Hey, we all have our cross to bear. I expect nothing but sympathy from you." She winks. "Come on. Chop, chop."

CHAPTER THIRTEEN

I've invited Caitlin to the nicest restaurant I've been to in my neighborhood. Sheryl took me and my fellow TA Mona to the Orange Tree to celebrate the end of the last academic year. When I arrive, I order a glass of mid-range Sauvignon Blanc. Tonight is not a night to pinch my pennies. I'll have a few more cup noodles meals the rest of the week.

By the time she arrives, I have a mild buzz going, and it makes her look even more perfect when she strides to our table. She's wearing tight beige pants with a jeans shirt tucked into the waistband. On me, an outfit like that would look casual—and ridiculous—but on Caitlin it looks glamorous and stylish.

I relish the quick touch of her lips against my cheek when she kisses me hello.

"At last," she says when she sits down. "We're doing this."

She orders a bottle of the wine I'm drinking then looks around. "Nice place. Must be new. I don't remember it from my uni days."

"It's been here for quite some time."

"Sometimes I forget how long I've been away. It's true what they say, you know? The older you get, the more quickly time flies. I know it makes me sound like a terrible cliché, but no cliché is truer than that one." She gives me a smile with those blood-red painted lips. "You're still so young. A minute is still actually a minute for you."

"And they can be excruciatingly slow sometimes."

The waiter brings over the bottle and Caitlin insists on pouring the wine herself.

"Do you miss it?" I ask, once we've toasted and held eye-contact for a split second. "America?"

"Much less than I had expected. I miss the few good friends I made, but these days, distance isn't the same as it used to be. You should see my inbox." She chuckles. "Some of them like to write really long emails. I prefer to save all those words for when I'm writing a book. Much better use of my time."

"Any news on the new book?"

She pulls her lips into a pout. "I have another meeting with the publisher next week. They need a bit more convincing, but I'm sure that will change as soon as I sign that contract with ANBC."

"Who knew your life abroad would be so easily replicated back home?" I sip from my wine.

"Not entirely replicated. I had a meeting with your esteemed Dean today. I told him I'd happily do a few guest lectures, but I don't want to go back to teaching. At least not in a university context. Too much admin." She brings a finger to her chin.

"You have TAs for that."

She quirks up her eyebrows. "I guess, but what a waste of intelligence." She slants her head a little. "But enough about me, Josephine. You've read my Wikipedia page. You know all there is to know about me. I want to know what your Wikipedia page would say."

"There's still plenty of stuff I don't know about you." I narrow my eyes. "Plenty."

"We'll get to that later then, once we've finished this." She fishes the wine bottle out of the ice bucket and tops up our glasses. "Please tell me something about you I don't know yet."

I shake my head. "That's not how conversation on a

date is supposed to flow."

"Oh, really? How is it supposed to *flow* then?" She briefly bites her bottom lip. "Or do I spot some reluctance to talk about yourself?"

"I don't know. You've achieved so much already. I'm just a girl who grades papers for Sheryl."

"I happen to believe you're much more than that. Besides, I would never hold your youth against you. And who's to say you won't have far surpassed my *achievements* by the time you're my age?"

The waiter stops by to take our order. We've barely looked at the menu. I'm not that hungry, but I should eat something to soak up all this wine we're having. We both end up ordering lamb chops.

"Where were we?" Caitlin asks. "Oh yes, the Josephine Greenwood Wikipedia page. If you could do whatever you wanted in the next decade, without impediments, what would it say in ten years' time?"

"I would definitely want to have written a book. In the same vein as the one by Ursula Attwell you gave me, but perhaps with more of a scientific research background. And I think I'd want to teach."

"You can take Sheryl's job when she retires."

"I'd never be as good as her. She's one of the most highly regarded professors of the entire university."

"There's no reason why you couldn't be. You're her protégée for a reason. Does she have you teach already?"

I nod. "Two classes a week."

"Are they open to visitors?" She gives me a wide smile. "I'd love to drop by."

"I'm sure no one would deny esteemed alumnus Caitlin James access."

"Would *you*?"

"I wouldn't dream of it." Although the thought of teaching in front of Caitlin terrifies me, this little lie fits too perfectly in our current flirtation.

"Where do I sign up?" Caitlin makes it sound as though she can't get enough of me. I'm still at a loss why. If she keeps looking at me like that, I'm much inclined to start believing her.

"Just swing by this Friday afternoon. We're talking about the impact of digital technologies on gender dynamics. Just don't intimidate the students too much."

"Ooh, Friday afternoon. The graveyard lecture."

"It has its advantages. Only really motivated students show up."

"Or the ones who really, really like you."

I chuckle. "I'm pretty sure none of them do."

"How can you know for certain?" Caitlin cocks her head again; her stare is intense. This is beginning to feel like a real, full-on date.

Our dishes arrive and she takes the opportunity to refill our glasses again. With the way she has been pouring, the bottle is empty already. She orders another.

———

"I have one sister," I reply when Caitlin asks me about my family.

"Younger or older? She can't possibly be cuter."

"Bea's ten years younger. Mum had her quite late. She has Down Syndrome. She's in a special school. I don't get to see her very often, but we talk every morning on the phone."

"That's so sweet, that you call her every day." Caitlin appears to be a very quick eater—a detail I was too flummoxed to notice at previous occasions—and she has polished off most of her dish already. As a result of the many diets I have tried, I chew my food slowly and most of my lamb chops are still on my plate. "Do you go home often?"

"I don't. Can't really afford the flight, to be honest." I recall Bea's pleading voice from the other day.

"Oh," is all Caitlin says and I hope she'll leave it there. I can't think of a more unsexy topic to discuss on this date than my finances.

"What about your family?" If nothing else, I'm the champion of conversation redirection.

"They're in Evanston, near Melbourne. We don't talk much."

I briefly consider not prying but I don't want to risk the topic returning to my financial situation. "How come?"

"Here's some information that's not on my Wikipedia page. They don't care much for what I do. Having a lesbian daughter was already hardship enough for them, but do I really need to shout it from the rooftops? It's safe to say I won't be going home any time soon either."

"That's rough. They can clearly see how successful you are."

"Some people only see what they want to see."

"Is it a religious thing or…"

"Just good old-fashioned bigotry." She pushes her plate away. "It's not just the fact that I'm a lesbian or that I'm so outspoken about women's rights. Perhaps they could have accepted it more if I behaved more along heteronormative expectations. Got myself a wife, a house, and two kids, but that's never been for me. My mother has even gone so far as to call me a slut. I subsequently sent her a copy of *The Ethical Slut*. The s-word incident has never been mentioned since."

"Ouch."

"How did your parents take it? Presuming you're out."

"They're not very worldly people—they only cross the town borders to visit my sister—but they have the biggest hearts. Life's not been easy on them so they know what's truly important. They just want me to be happy, even though I've yet to introduce them to a girlfriend."

"It's great that they're so accepting."

"I think it hurt them more that I chose Gender Studies when I got my scholarship. I was always the smartest girl in class and they had high hopes for me. Despite not having had many chances themselves, they always told me I could become whatever I wanted when I grew up, and this is what I chose. It was stronger than any desire to make a lot of money and make all of our lives better in the process."

"I'm sure they're secretly very proud of you."

"My dad is a very intelligent man, but his family didn't have money for higher education. His father had a menial job lined up for him with the town council as soon as he finished high school, so that's what he did until he hurt his back in an accident. He's been on disability ever since. The fact that I'm an academic must please him on some level, but he has another, less fortunate daughter to worry about. I wanted Bea to go to a school where she would be treated as a normal person, so I'm paying for it by working at the Pink Bean. Every single cent I earn goes to Bea's education."

"You're a good person, just like your parents."

"I just want to do right by my sister."

"I'm sure she adores you."

"She's the sweetest person you'll ever meet. I admit, sometimes it's hard to call her at seven o'clock every single morning, but the second I hear her voice, it always perks me up. She has that effect on me. It's like she has sunshine in her voice. She's almost always in a good mood and even when she's not, it doesn't take a lot to cheer her up." I put my cutlery down. "I miss her. And sometimes I wish I had chosen to study for an MBA and I had a well-paid corporate job by now. One that would allow me to fly home for every holiday and for Bea's birthday, but some things you just have to do for yourself. I never could imagine myself going to work in a business suit every day, poring over spreadsheets and *working for the man*."

"Well, the next special occasion you wish you'd been able to fly home, just come to mine and I'll throw you an alternate party."

"That's very kind of you."

"Says the woman who is the very definition of

kindness."

I wave Caitlin off. She smiles at me.

"Dessert?" she asks.

"I'm not much of a dessert person."

"Well, I am." She starts looking around for the waiter. She orders a chocolate fondant with two spoons and pours more wine. Despite the meal I just ate, I'm feeling pretty lightheaded.

"No meal is complete without dessert," Caitlin says.

"Maybe in your world, but when your own mother told you from a very young age that it would probably benefit you to forego the pavlova she made, your thoughts might differ."

"She didn't?"

"I can't even blame her for it. She only ever believed she had my best interests at heart."

"But still. That's a harsh thing to say to a child."

"Not when your child weighs twice as much as most of her class mates."

Caitlin shakes her head, pouts her lips. "That must have made you feel awful."

I shrug. "I believed her. Just as I believed my classmates when they called me a hippo. I was a child. I didn't know any better."

"I'm really sorry that happened to you." Caitlin puts a hand on the table and scoots it in my direction.

"It was a long time ago."

"More often than not, it's the things that happened the longest ago that stay with us for the rest of our lives."

I inch my hand a little closer to hers. I sneak a glance at her long, slender fingers, her red-painted nails. "I think it's time to change the subject," I say on a sigh.

"Okay. I think I was just about to say something patronizing anyway." Caitlin draws her lips into a lop-sided smile. Her hand remains on the table. "Your turn to ask me anything."

I look at my glass of wine. Take another sip. I have many pressing questions that can't just be asked outright but need to be worked toward in the delicate back-and-forth of an intimate conversation. But I've drunk a lot of wine and Caitlin's hand is lying less than an inch away from mine. I think I have permission.

"How long did the longest relationship you've had last?"

She breathes out a loud chuckle. "My reputation does precede me, then."

"I'm just curious." A blush warms my neck.

"Fair enough." She narrows her eyes to slits. "Her name was Michelle. We were together for three and a half years. She lived in New York and I lived in Boston. It was kind of a long-distance thing, though I did spend a lot of time at her place in New York."

"Why did it end?" I'm not sure if I'm baiting her. If I am, I'm sure she's on to me.

"The same reasons most of my relationships have ended. Irreconcilable differences on the structure and boundaries of a long-term relationship."

"What's your view on them?"

She gives a small laugh. "I've written extensively on how I believe that monogamy is an archaic invention by the patriarchy, with a ridiculous double standard attached to it, and only meant to keep women in check. I won't give you a big speech on what you already know."

"I'm pretty well-versed in all the arguments for and against non-monogamous relationships. Ten years in the Gender Studies department will do that to you."

"It's still frowned upon, though. It's still called cheating or, worse, being unfaithful. Have you ever stopped to really consider that term? *Faithful?* It doesn't have any bearing on what a relationship really is." She shrugs. "Everyone is different and entitled to their own opinion, of course, but I just always thought that when 2016 came around, things would be different. I guess that's what I miss most about the States. The people I hung out with who didn't give a rat's ass about conforming to societal norms. What a glorious gang of misfits. The word may have a negative connotation for most, but for me, there's no bigger compliment than being called a misfit."

"I feel like a misfit about eighty-five percent of the time."

"Then we are kindred souls, Josephine. By the way, I really love your name. It's beautiful and it really, really suits you."

"Thank you." I smile sheepishly and hold Caitlin's gaze for a split second. Her glance doesn't waver. We're reaching the final—or perhaps penultimate, though my mind can't really go there—act of our date. I can tell. The intensity is being ratcheted up. Locked gazes prolonged. Intentions almost stated.

The moment passes when the waiter brings dessert accompanied by two spoons.

———

"I know that, officially, this is our first date, but we've spent quite some time together already, haven't we?" Caitlin says before licking the last fleck of chocolate from her lips. I let her have most of the dessert, only dipping my spoon in ceremoniously a few times. Some compulsions are hard to break.

"We have. And I've enjoyed every single minute of getting to know you better."

"Really? Even that time when you blew me off?"

I wave her off. "Oh that. That's in the past now, Forgotten. Bygones."

Caitlin gives me a smile that lights up her entire face. "Deal. That never happened."

We sit in silence for a split second.

"Can I make you another deal?" Caitlin asks.

"Sure."

"Let me pay for the meal. In return, invite me back to your place. For coffee or for whatever you want. I'm not willing for the evening to end just yet."

Eva would have a fit if I walked in with Caitlin while she and Declan are canoodling in our rickety sofa. "Counter offer," I say. "Let's split the bill and we can go to yours."

Caitlin scrunches her lips together. "Accepted." She looks around to signal to the waiter that we are ready for the check.

CHAPTER FOURTEEN

"Welcome to my place, again," Caitlin says. "One day, you'll show me yours." On the way over, in the back of an Uber—of course—I explained profusely why it was a bad idea to go to mine.

"I promise." I stand around awkwardly while Caitlin switches on a few dimmed lights. I still have a good wine buzz going and more confidence than I ought to have in this situation.

"Can I offer you another drink?"

"I truly think I've had enough." I head over to the big sofa. "And I have an early start tomorrow."

"You can text Micky. Tell her you'll be in a bit later." There's mischief in Caitlin's voice.

"No way. She knows where I am right now. I'll never live it down. Besides, Micky is not my boss. Kristin is."

We both sit down. As always, no matter how tipsy I am, I flex all my muscles, hoping in vain it will make my weight press down less into the cushions.

"Kristin will understand," Caitlin says.

"She will understand what exactly?"

Caitlin has shuffled close to me. I can feel the fabric of her pants through the flimsy cotton of my dress.

"You came all the way to Darlinghurst. Which, at the very least, gives me permission to do this." She angles her body toward me, cups my cheeks in her hands, and pulls me close. Before she closes her eyes and kisses me, she gazes into mine.

Oh Christ. I can't believe this is happening. The entire evening has been leading up to this. Of course I came all this way with this in mind. But still, I can't quite believe it. I feel like I've landed in the middle of a dream, a fantasy I really shouldn't have.

When her lips press against mine, my body tenses up even more. It's not hesitation making me clamp up—because, oh how I've wanted to kiss Caitlin—it's the voice in my head telling me this whole scene is ridiculous.

"Are you all right?" she asks with genuine concern in her voice.

"Can't quite believe it," I whisper.

She smiles, the skin around her eyes scrunching up. "It's very, very real." Her hands are still on my cheeks and she pulls me close again. Before she presses her lips to mine, she asks, "Can I kiss you again, Josephine?"

I have to giggle at the formality of it. "Please."

This time, her tongue slips past my lips and I relax into our embrace, bringing my hands to her sides. This is really going to happen. I may not be very experienced at this, but this is not the kind of kiss that will just fade into nothing. The intensity of it sparks up my spine, makes me forget who I am for an instant—makes me forget that I really shouldn't rush this.

She catches my bottom lip between her teeth, gives it a soft tug before setting it free and looking at me. "I'm glad you came all this way. Will you stay?"

I just nod, afraid even the word *yes* can't make it past the lump in my throat. I want her so much. Surely, with Caitlin, things will be different.

"Come on." She rises and offers her hand. I let her pull me out of the sofa. "I'd like to show you my bedroom."

Hand in hand, we walk to the other wing of this ridiculously large apartment. I try to steady my breathing to no avail. In unguarded moments, I've entertained the notion of this happening, but no sooner had I conjured up the thought, than I banned it to that zone of unthinkable thoughts somewhere in the back of my brain. In the cold light of day, Caitlin and I don't make any sense. But it's evening. We've been on an amazing date. She makes me feel wanted, sexy even. In this moment, it does make sense, and this moment is all that matters.

I don't notice the decor of her bedroom. I'm sure it's swanky and cozy and luscious, but I'm not interested in anything but Caitlin's lips on mine again. In tugging that blouse out of her pants and riding my hands up her back, in feeling her skin react to my touch.

Our lips meet again and again and by the time my mouth is smeared in her lipstick and my hair has come undone because of her hands rummaging through it, I have my fingers underneath her blouse. She feels so tiny in my hands, so brittle, so unlike anything I've ever felt before.

"Let's lie down," she says, then hoists her blouse over her head and tosses it onto a chair.

Oh damn, time to disrobe. I take a split second to remember this is Caitlin. I can communicate with her. I can tell her that I'm not comfortable being totally naked in front of her.

"Can I undo that zipper?" she asks, bringing her hands to my back. This dress is all that separates my body from Caitlin's gaze. I feel like I have an urgent decision to make. Let go or hold on. I choose to let go. I choose to risk it all with Caitlin.

I nod.

She spins me around, presses a hair-raising kiss to the nape of my neck, then slowly unzips my dress. My skin reacts to the air of the room by breaking out in goosebumps.

My body is not a surprise to her, I tell myself. A second-hand polka-dot dress doesn't cover a damn thing. Still, it's daunting to stand there, my dress pooled at my feet. Caitlin's gaze burning my back. I should turn around, face her, but I can't. Instead, I kick the dress away, flip back the quilt on the bed, and slide underneath, my back still to her.

I hear rustling behind me. I try to take a few deep breaths, try to enjoy the moment for what it is.

Turn around, the voice in my head goes.

By the time I muster up the courage to face Caitlin again, she slips under the covers with me, wearing just her bra and panties.

"Hey," she says, as her warm hands find mine underneath the sheets. "I want you, Josephine. I like you and I think you're beautiful."

I reply by inching closer and peppering kisses on her cheek, along the line of her exquisite cheekbone, then down to her mouth, which opens so easily, so greedily for me, it takes away another layer of inhibition. It's been a long time since I've let another woman under the sheets with me. Even if nothing else happens tonight, this is already a big victory for me. But who am I kidding? My heart is pounding, my skin sizzling. I want her just as badly. I push Caitlin back into the pillows and look at her for an instant before kissing her again. Nothing in her face says she doesn't want me in her bed. Nothing about her has ever given me any other impression than that she does genuinely like me. She asked me out. This is the third time she has invited me into her home. It was never Caitlin who needed convincing; it was always me. Because of the doubts that are such an integral part of me; they're always there. Even when my mouth finds hers again, and our tongues dance around, and the grip of her hands becomes more insistent, the doubts aren't banished that easily. A lifetime of them will do that to you.

To overcome them, I'm going to have to take charge. To reach that level of extreme lust, of no going back, I'm going to need the confidence that will, I hope, engulf me after I've made her come.

While our lips keep meeting, and our kisses grow more frantic, I try to get a hand beneath Caitlin's back to unsnap her bra. She helps me by arching up. It only takes a little bit of fumbling to relieve her of the garment. And then I feast my eyes on Caitlin's naked chest. Her breasts are small, with tiny nipples—the complete opposite of mine. The contrast strangely turns me on and I can't help myself. I need to take them into my mouth pronto. Need to taste that part of her. Need to flick my tongue over her pert nipples, and lose myself a little bit more.

Her nipples appear very sensitive and she arches her back again, pushing herself into me, a moan escaping her in between ragged breaths.

I trace my lips down to her belly button, flicking my tongue inside, then up again, needing her mouth again, needing her to breathe into me.

"I want you so much," she repeats when we break from our kiss. "God, I'm so ready."

She all but pushes me down. I happily oblige. Caitlin's hands gently nudging me, her fingers hot on the skin of my shoulders, is a sensation I'll never forget. Because it makes clear exactly how much she wants me. And oh, do I want it too.

I crawl down, taking most of the covers with me. I block the thought of what I must look like to her, on my hands and knees like that, and focus on what I'm about to do. Give Caitlin the highest pleasure—I hope.

She's already pushing her panties down. I guide them off her legs and throw them somewhere into the semi-darkness, which I'm very grateful for. She spreads her legs wide for me, displaying no qualms, only pure desire. I'm not sure I've ever really come across the very picture of raw lust like this. Part of me finds it hard to believe that I inspired it, but the evidence is undeniable.

I look at her, I have to. Before I kiss her there, I need to see the most intimate part of her. Need to acquaint myself and etch it in my memory forever. I don't know where this will end. I might be in bed with her, but the chance of me actually embarking on anything resembling a relationship with Caitlin remains small. This is just sex. She's not that much into relationships, anyway. We have so much left to talk about. I have so many questions left to ask her. There's so much more of her to know, but right now, it's boiled down to this very essence: me looking at her while she waits for me to go down on her. Caitlin at her most animalistic. At her most pure.

I can't wait any longer. I plant a kiss just below her belly button, then make my way down. Her pubic hair is neatly trimmed—did she do that with this in mind? Or does she keep it this neat all the time?— and tickles my nose as I go lower.

"Josephine," she moans. "Please."

Never in my wildest dreams had I imagined Caitlin to beg me like this. It ignites my own lust. Her desire will spur mine on, will take me to where she is now. Ready. No doubts. Total surrender.

I let my tongue skate along her sex, her wetness is salty on my lips. The tip of my tongue skates lightly against her clit, but her limbs stiffen anyway. To see such desire on display makes my own clit throb between my legs. She seems so sensitive, so overly ready, as though the entire night was foreplay. Oh, to be carefree like that. But really, here I am, about as free as I've ever been. Never have I gone to bed with someone after the first date. It was never even a speck of a possibility. Who could ever garner that kind of lust for me without knowing me better?

Spurred on by the motions of her body and the groans coming from her mouth, I let my tongue dance around her clit. Her hands find my hair again, twisting long strands of it around her fingers. But I feel no pain, only the will to make her come, to do that very thing to her that makes her surrender, give herself up to me.

I suck her clit between my lips, let my tongue swirl over it more. Then I'm overtaken with my own desire. I want to feel her. I take a little breather and while doing so, spread her lips wide with my fingers, take another good look at her, then, slowly, gently, push a finger inside of her.

"Oh, fuck," Caitlin groans and the sound of her voice shot through with lust and joy like that, with me as the cause for them, adds another layer to my already growing confidence.

My finger is being enveloped by her warm wetness, by the evidence of her lust for me and as I delve deeper, find a rhythm, bring my tongue back into the game, for an instant, I believe that this very moment has undone a lifetime of shame and hating my body. Because look at where I am and what I'm doing. Nothing will ever beat this—except, perhaps, a repeat performance.

Caitlin reacts to my thrusts by bucking up her hips violently and pushing her fingernails into my scalp.

"Oh Christ," she whispers. "Oh, yes. Oh, yes."

I add another finger and luxuriate in the feel of her, in the sensation of being as inside of her as any person could ever be, in the exquisite intimacy of the moment. But still, there's that ever-nagging voice in the back of my mind: will it be enough?

Caitlin climaxes with a loud, syncopated moan, her palms pressing hard against my skull, my fingers clenched together inside of her.

"Oh, fuck," she says when her body relaxes, setting me free, and she sinks back into the mattress.

I'm looking around for something to wipe my hand with, but she pulls me to her by my arm, and says, "Come here." She takes the hand I fucked her with in hers and brings my fingers to her lips, then proceeds to suck her own juices from them.

The sight of Caitlin's lips wrapped around my fingers unleashes something in my core, peels off a layer of inhibition. She seems so free of the thoughts that continuously plague me, so assured in her post-orgasmic glow, it's infectious. I remember what Caitlin said about seeing something of her past self in me. Right now, I hope I'm looking at my future. Near and distant.

"I guess I needed that," she says after she lets my fingers slip from her mouth. She turns on her side. "It's been a while."

I'm curious to know how long exactly, but this is not the moment to ask.

"Thank you," she says.

"There's really no need to thank me," I stammer.

"Of course there is. I strongly believe if we all thanked our lovers a bit more, the world would be a better place." She laughs a throaty laugh. "Now." She runs a finger over my arm. "Tell me what you like, Josephine."

What I like? There goes the confidence I'd built up while being allowed all over—and inside—her.

"Much the same as you, I think."

"Hm," she hums, while her finger scoots from my upper arm to where my breasts spill out of my bra. "You think?"

"I—I'm not really comfortable talking about, er, this," I manage to say, while I feel my body tensing up under her touch.

"So you're just going to let me run wild?" She presses her lips against my shoulder. "Are you sure about that?"

I suck my bottom lip into my mouth and just nod.

"Okay." Her finger has dipped into the tight crevasse between my breasts. It must be so hot and sweaty there. Part of me wants so desperately to take off my bra already, but the other, more prevailing part wants to hide some more.

I need to stop thinking like this. Need to just give myself up to Caitlin and her intention to, basically, do whatever she wants to me. I try to conjure up the state of mind when I'm alone in bed and I can only imagine her doing this to me. Why is that so much more effective?

"Relax, Josephine." My name is but a whisper on her

lips. "Everything will be all right. You're in good hands." She chuckles then slips a leg over me. "I'm going to take off your bra now," she whispers in my ear.

"Okay." The bra I'm wearing is the closest to an alluring piece of lingerie I can find in my size. Compared to the bra I put on for running, it's a big step up on the sexiness scale, but next to the flimsy thing I helped Caitlin out of earlier, it still looks more like a stringent corset for my breasts than anything else. I could hardly have them hanging on my belly for this date.

Like all of my bras, this one opens at the front and it takes a bit of finesse to unhook, but Caitlin takes her time and, ever so slowly, frees my breasts from their cage. They tumble out and I can't help but sigh a little with relief. There's never a better moment in my day than coming home and taking off my bra.

Immediately, Caitlin brings her mouth to one of my nipples and takes it between her lips. She takes her time lavishing attention on my breasts, leaving my nipples rock hard peaks by the time she focuses her attention elsewhere.

As enthralling as it is to have her mouth all over me— trailing down my belly right now—I find it impossible to forget about my body. When I look down, it's there looming like a vast white fleshy mass. Like something not made for this kind of pleasure.

Caitlin spreads my legs and kisses me over the fabric of my panties, which coaxes an involuntary groan from my throat. If only, I keep thinking. If only I wasn't so me.

I let her take off my undies and let her do all the things I did to her, but despite the insistent flick of her tongue over my clit, and the push of her fingers inside my wet, wet sex, I can't meld the thought of her making love to me with her actually doing it. There's a chasm in my mind that makes it impossible for my body to go past that plateau. I make all the right noises and I take as much pleasure as I can get, for Caitlin's fingers inside of me are definitely a source of delight, but I know, as certain as I know my name is Josephine Greenwood, that I won't be able to come. I've never been able to at the hands of anyone else—only my own. I was a fool to think it would be different with Caitlin.

I try to enjoy a few more strokes of her long, agile fingers inside of me, but then I start preparing for the inevitable moment of shame. Tapping Caitlin on the shoulder and telling her all her efforts were in vain.

I glance down and take in the image of her crouched between my legs one last time—ironically, I know it will serve me well later, when I'm all alone in my own bed.

"Caitlin," I whisper, putting a hand on her shoulder.

She looks up immediately. "Are you okay?" she asks. Her fingers are still inside of me and are beginning to feel like they don't belong—like an intrusion.

"Just, er, stop for a second."

"Okay." Slowly, she lets her fingers slip from me and unceremoniously wipes them on the sheets. "What's wrong?" she asks once she has crawled up to me.

"It's definitely not you." Oh God, what do I even say? No matter what comes out of my mouth, it will make me sound lame and immature and like a fraud—who am I to write my thesis on body acceptance when being in bed naked with another woman freaks me out to this extent?

"It's okay, Josephine. Just talk to me. Tell me what you'd like me to do."

I shake my head. "I don't want you to do anything, just… er, understand. I'm…" *I'm what?*

"These things happen for all sorts of reasons. The main thing is that you don't worry about it too much," she says. "And don't you dare worry about me either, my ego is not that fragile that it gets dented when I fail to get a woman off."

"It's not you," I repeat. "I'm in my head too much."

"I happen to believe that a woman's climax is her own responsibility, but it doesn't mean we can't talk about it so that, perhaps, next time, you can start getting a bit closer."

Next time? Surely there will be no next time after this. Caitlin can theorize all she wants. She can give a hundred reasons why this is normal and nothing to be ashamed of, it won't change how I feel. Mortified. Unworthy. Strengthened in my belief that me in Caitlin's bed is a farce. I should have stuck with my initial gut instinct and never have let this date happen.

"Talk to me," she insists.

I don't want to talk. "I should probably go." My body remains immovable in her bed.

"Stay." She slings an arm over my torso. "We don't have to talk. We don't have to do anything you don't want to. Just, give me an inkling of how you're feeling. Just one word. That's all I ask."

"I feel like a failure," I say, fighting back tears. Oh no, I'm not going to cry in Caitlin's bed. There's just no way.

"Oh, Josephine." She kisses me on the cheek. "You're nothing of the sort. You're still so young. Don't for a second think that not being able to have an orgasm when you sleep with someone, for the very first time I may add, is not normal. Ask ten random women and you'll quickly know how common it is. It's nothing to be ashamed of or to feel like a failure about."

"That's just the thing. I should know better. I shouldn't beat myself up over it. It's not as if I didn't know it was going to be like this, but still. I can't help how I feel."

"But you tried. You plucked up the courage to ask me out again and to come home with me. There's a lot to be said for that."

"Is there?"

"Of course." She presses herself closer to me. "Please don't go."

The thought of having to make my way home is, in fact, more daunting than staying in Caitlin's warm bed, listening to her soothing words.

"Okay, I'll stay." There's not much chance of me catching any sleep at all—I haven't slept in the same bed with anyone in quite a few years.

"Good." She rests her head in the crook of my arm, then lets a finger linger over my breast. "We can try again in a while, if you like,"

"No." My tone is too snappy and curt and I regret it instantly. "I'm sorry." I pull her a little closer. "I just wish things could have been different."

"They will be. Trust me."

What does that mean? Does she mean with her? Or in the future, with someone else? And how would she know?

"Can I get you anything? Some water? A night cap?" Her voice sounds sleepy.

"I'm fine." I kiss her on the top of her head. I think of my clothes strewn across the room—and of the audacity I had when I was getting ready for this date, when I slipped a clean pair of knickers into my purse.

"Will you be able to sleep?" she mumbles.

"Sure," I lie.

"Good night." A few minutes later, Caitlin's breathing slows and she breaks out into the lightest of purrs.

CHAPTER FIFTEEN

I must have dozed off at some point in the night, because I wake up lying on my stomach with my leg hanging halfway out of Caitlin's bed. There's an alarm clock on her side so I push myself up to see the time. It's 5:45 a.m. I'm relieved I got some sleep and conclude it must have been sheer emotional exhaustion that knocked me out in the end.

I try not to move too much so as not to wake up Caitlin. I wish I had found a way to sneak my running shoes into my purse so I could go for a jog, to run all the negative feelings that still bloom inside my chest off me. I briefly consider making my way back to Camperdown and get a set of clean clothes and just be by myself for a little while, but dinner last night was expensive and a return bus fare, when I have to come back to Darlinghurst for my shift at the Pink Bean anyway, seems like a silly expense.

I glance over at Caitlin and remember how her body felt in my hands. So willing, so much along the line of expectations. She's lying on her back, the covers pulled all the way up to her chin, as though she's protecting me from her nakedness—or herself from my prying eyes.

Ironically, a surge of lust sweeps through me at the sight of her sleeping, relaxed face. Her lipstick is smudged and her mascara has left black flecks on her temples.

She was so sweet last night, said all the right things, but I can't imagine a woman like Caitlin not being a little bit offended by my failure to climax. Though I'm not sure what

I actually mean by *a woman like Caitlin*. A woman who has had many lovers? A woman who believes sexual pleasure should not be contained within the confines of a relationship? Again, as I lie next to her in bed, the thought strikes me that we couldn't be more different.

I roll onto my back, careful not to stir the mattress too much, and I get a tickle in my throat. My mouth is dry as an aftereffect of all that wine last night and I decide to fetch some water.

I walk through Caitlin's apartment naked. I could have scurried for my dress in the darkness of the bedroom, but Caitlin's apartment is so high up, no one could possibly look inside and see me.

I head to the kitchen, fill a glass with water, and drink greedily. I can still smell her on me as I bring the glass to my mouth. I walk to the bookshelves that impressed me so much the first time I came here—did she already want to sleep with me then?—and run a finger over the spines. All these works on feminism, body acceptance, and the role of women throughout history, and here I am, feeling so diminished by my inability to come at Caitlin's hands.

She's probably right that many women suffer the same fate, but I bet that most of these women don't have the other problem that I have. The very thing I walk around in, that I see with every glimpse in the mirror or reflection of a shop window. Of course, the problem lies with me; the me in relation to the others. All the others who see me as lazy and morally depraved because of how I look.

My legs are restless. I already miss not being able to go for my run. It's the only thing that can reset me when I'm in a negative thought spiral. Those dreadful moments when I sincerely believe that it *is* all my own fault, that I should have more character, should go on yet another diet—as if I haven't tried them all and every last one of them hasn't failed me more than the previous one. That I should just become a better version of myself already—as if it were that easy.

Maybe I can call Bea early today, but she won't like it. She's such a stickler for routine.

Caitlin's place is air-conditioned and a shiver runs up my spine. Either I crawl back under the covers with her or I take a shower and surprise Kristin by showing up at the Pink Bean an hour early for my shift.

"Hey." Caitlin's voice comes from the end of the hallway. "For a minute there, I thought you'd left."

"Nowhere to go," I say, rather dramatically.

"Is it so bad here?" Caitlin is as naked as I am.

"No." I swallow a hint of tightness out of my throat.

"Come back to bed for a bit?" She looks angelic in the burgeoning light.

I nod and follow her back to the bedroom.

"Hey," she says again and shuffles close to me under the covers. My hands are cold and she takes them in hers, warming them. "Did you get some sleep?"

"I did. I'm sorry if I woke you."

"I'm an early riser, no matter what I did the night before." She chuckles.

"Must be your age," I joke.

"Watch it." She squeezes my fingers between her hands. "I had a great time last night," she says.

"Me too."

"Would you like to do it again some time?" Caitlin looks so unlike her when she asks it. So defenseless and vulnerable. Almost endearing enough to make me blindly say yes.

"I—I'm not sure that would be a good idea." I look away.

"Don't blow me off a second time, Josephine. I can kind of tell that you like me." She brings my hands to her mouth, kisses a knuckle. "Is this about your lost climax?"

Lost climax? Is that what we're calling it now?

"No, well, yes, a bit." If only more and more sunlight wasn't streaming into Caitlin's bedroom, I could hide better.

"Do you think it's the first time I've slept with someone who wasn't able to come? Or that it has never happened to me? Female sexuality is complex."

I know Caitlin means well, but I can't have this conversation again. She may think that, in time, everything will be all right, but she doesn't know why my two previous relationships ended.

"Can we talk about something else, please?"

"If you answer my question first." She presses my hands against her warm chest. "Will you go out with me again?"

"Am I some sort of pity project for you? Or do you get a weird kick out of dating a fat girl?" I pull my hands from hers. "I think I'll take a shower now."

I look at her flabbergasted face for an instant, then turn around and sit at the edge of the bed with my back to her. I could not be dealing with this in a worse manner.

"I'm sorry. I didn't meant to snap," I mumble. I look around for something to wrap my body in, to hide myself away with.

"We'll talk later," Caitlin says. "I'll stop by the Pink Bean."

I remain seated for a few seconds longer, hoping to feel a reconciliatory hand on my back, but I remain untouched. I'm well aware that it's not Caitlin who has amends to make. But she doesn't know what it's like to be trapped in my body, this extra-padded shell I have to go through life with. She doesn't know that not a day goes by that I don't get a stare or a comment or, worst of all, a look of pity.

To her, it might be about me not being able to reach the level of surrender to have an orgasm at her hand, but to me, it's about so much more.

I can't find anything to wrap myself in for my walk of shame to the bathroom, but there's just no way I'm walking out of her bedroom naked. My legs won't function unless I have camouflage. Without looking behind me, I pull the sheet that's under the quilt off the bed and use it to cover myself up.

As I walk to the ensuite bathroom, which is just a few steps away from where I was sitting, I conclude that I was always too messed up to date the likes of Caitlin James.

———

I call Bea on the way to the Pink Bean. After our usual greeting, she says, "You sound a bit sad, JoJo."

"I'm just a little tired, that's all. Nothing for you to worry about." I try to reassure her. The last thing I want is my sister to worry about me. For anyone to worry about me. There's plenty of me to worry about me, I think.

"Is it because you won't see me for my birthday?" she asks, disregarding my comment.

"Yes. That makes me very sad. But we'll have an extra long Skype call that day, so you'll be able to see my face and I'll be able to see yours."

"Then I can show you my presents," she says. "I think I know what I'm going to get."

While I stand in front of the Pink Bean window, we chat a little more. Today, not even my sister's voice seems to be able to cheer me up.

CHAPTER SIXTEEN

"Still in your party dress, I see," Micky says as soon as she sees me. "Must have been a good night."

I have to spend the next four and a half hours with her in a confined space, so I take a deep breath before I reply. I don't want to snap at her, I've done enough of that already and it's only eight o'clock.

And really, up until fifteen minutes before we went to sleep, it *was* a perfect night.

"Come on, Jo. Don't keep us in suspense." Micky is not one to let something like this go. Never mind that I gave her all the space she so obviously needed when she'd just started dating Robin and she didn't know which way was up.

Kristin is setting up the chairs around the tables and just as I'm about to say something just to satisfy Micky, Sheryl comes down. *Great.*

"I need to go in early today," she says, "any chance of a quick fix before I go?" I could kiss her for detracting attention from me, but I also wish I could get into her car with her and go to the university to hide away in my office. I can't go home because Eva will be full of questions as well.

"Of course." I prepare Sheryl's espresso and take the time to come up with something to say about the date. What will Caitlin say to Sheryl? Will she discount what happened this morning and relay it as a good one?

"Didn't you have your date with Caitlin last night?" She eyes my dress. "Still in fancy clothes, I see. I know what that means." She winks as I hand her the coffee. "You spent the night in Darlinghurst."

I expel a sigh, then say, "Please, everyone listen because I'm only going to say this once. It was a good date and yes, to satisfy your overly curious minds"—I shoot Micky a look —"I did spend the night. But that's all I'm going to say about it. I don't want to talk about it any more and I hope you'll respect my privacy."

For a split second, Micky looks taken aback, then she says, in the sulking way I've heard her teenage daughter use, "Fine."

"Are you okay?" Sheryl asks. She is the champion of reading between the lines, after all. She figured out I needed to make some more money and got me this job. She rearranged my schedule so I could work at the Pink Bean every weekday morning and had me tell her about Bea only days after I became her TA and wasn't comfortable talking about that to my boss at all.

"I'm fine. Just, you know, I don't think there will be any follow-up dates."

"Come here." Sheryl waves two fingers at me.

I walk over to the side of the counter.

"Did Caitlin treat you all right? Because if she didn't, I *will* have a word with her."

"It's nothing like that. She was nothing but gracious. We're just not very, er, suited for each other, that's all. Nothing for you to worry about." I can't believe I'm actually needing to have this conversation with my boss. "I'll see you this afternoon."

"Understood," Sheryl says. She kisses Kristin on the lips and heads out.

Only two more sets of prying eyes to deal with. I'm not worried about Kristin, who is as discreet and disciplined as they come. Micky, on the other hand, is going to grill me all morning long.

———

As promised, Caitlin stops by the Pink Bean at her usual time. By then, Micky has made a couple of remarks, but we've been blissfully busy and she hasn't had time to grill me too much.

"Did she pull an Amber on you?" she asked, after Kristin had gone upstairs and it was just us in the shop for a few minutes. "You know, told you it was just a one-night stand when you woke up this morning?"

That's another thing that confused me about Caitlin. Why would she even ask me to go out again? It can only be because she felt like I was unfinished business to her. A fat girl in need of a boost to her confidence. So she could heroically be the woman who rescues me from my own grim thoughts.

"Do you have time for a quick chat? I'm meeting Zoya here in fifteen minutes," Caitlin asks after she has ordered her flat white.

"Go on," Micky urges. "Honestly, Jo, you look like you need that chat."

I stop myself from asking Micky what the hell she means by that, and join Caitlin at her table by the window.

"I'm sorry you felt the need to leave so abruptly this morning," Caitlin says. "I must have pushed a very wrong button."

I look at her. She looks so drop dead gorgeous again. A flash of memory flits through my mind. My finger slipping inside. The noise she made when she came.

"I'm sorry for leaving like that. It wasn't very mature." I twirl my coffee cup between my fingers and stare at it intensely, afraid to confront her gaze. "I did have a really nice time, Caitlin. You mustn't think that I don't like you. There are just certain things… I don't know. I'm not ready for, I guess."

Caitlin purses her lips together. She's not wearing any lipstick today. "I would so like to ask you to trust me, but I know that's impossible."

"Trust you to do what?"

Inside my chest, anger wars with a surge of pure lust I feel just from sitting across from her.

"Trust me to guide you to where you want to be." She slants her head over the table. "Have you ever really trusted anyone?"

Is this turning into an impromptu counseling session now? "What does that have to do with anything?"

"Don't answer me now, just think about it. I'd like to take you out again. We don't have to do the whole restaurant thing. We can just get a takeout and eat it on my balcony. I would like to spend some more time with you, but I know that you're in a state right now and not very inclined to say yes. That's fine. That's why I'm asking you to take some time to think about it. I have time. I'm not going anywhere. Okay?" She looks up.

"Am I interrupting?" I look up and see Zoya. She's early and clearly not reading the situation well.

Again, I get the feeling that I don't belong in this chair, talking to Caitlin who is waiting for her newscaster friend. I might not have been perfectly happy before Caitlin started showing up at the Pink Bean, but at least I was content, at peace. I had my job at the university and my job here. It was enough. Look at me now. I'm about to fall to pieces because of Caitlin.

She rises to hug Zoya. It's just a hug among friends, yet I feel a pang of jealousy burrow its way up my chest. The other, even louder, thought crowding my brain is that Caitlin hugging someone like Zoya makes much more sense than her investing any more time in me. They are two beautiful, successful women, not a mismatched pair like Caitlin and I would make.

"Hi Josephine. Good to see you again." Zoya turns to Caitlin. "Were you talking about the book proposal? Because I have a few things to say about that as well."

Caitlin shakes her head. "Haven't got to that part yet."

Ah. The book. Probably the real reason why Caitlin is trying to keep me close. The subject didn't even come up last night. That's why she wants another date. She hasn't had a chance to ask me what she needs.

"I'll leave you to it." I feel ridiculous with my Pink Bean apron over my dress. I always wear jeans at work. The dress only reminds me of last night and makes me feel even more out of place.

"Promise me you'll think about it." Caitlin cocks her head.

"Okay," I say, even though I've made up my mind already.

———

"I know I can be a pain in the ass, but are you sure you're all right?" Micky asks.

Zoya and Caitlin are still sitting at their table, consumed by an animated conversation that seems to be cause for many eruptions of loud laughter.

Before I can even think about it, I blurt out, "I fucked up with Caitlin last night."

"How do you mean?" Micky is stacking cups into the dishwasher.

"I really don't want to talk about it. I know I'm a big old mope today. Tomorrow will be better, I promise."

"Do you want to come to mine for lunch after our shift? I have a huge batch of leftover mac and cheese." She straightens her posture.

"I really need to get home. I need to get out of these clothes."

"Are you sure?"

"I appreciate the offer and I will gladly take a rain check." I look down at my dress. "All this stupid dress reminds me of is last night. I just want to get back into my regular clothes and routine."

"Why don't you go home now. Our shift is almost over and I can handle things until Alyssa comes in. I'll tell Kristin you were feeling unwell."

The prospect of being able to leave the Pink Bean—and no longer having to look at Caitlin and be reminded of my inadequacies—is tempting, but I'm not one to leave a shift early.

"You're not so bad after all." I shoot Micky a grin. "It's okay. I'll stay."

CHAPTER SEVENTEEN

It's Friday afternoon and I'm about to start my lecture when the classroom door opens. Caitlin peeks her head in.

"I'm sorry I'm late," she says, though she looks more pleased with herself than apologetic. "Is it still okay for me to sit in?"

The students know very well who Caitlin is and most of them just stare at her open-mouthed, while one whoops and Nicole, the most outspoken one, says, "I saved you a seat right here, Miss James."

"Wonderful," Caitlin ambles in and sits next to Nicole.

This is just perfect. Not only is it very hard to keep the class' attention on a Friday afternoon, but now they'll be even more riled up and eager to start their weekend. But that's not the worst of it, of course. I love teaching, but having to do so in front of Caitlin, who has seen me naked and at my lowest, is pretty daunting.

"Okay," I say. "I was saving the debate on the power of television to affect acceptance of sexual diversity for next week. But seeing as we have a special guest, why not take advantage of Miss James' knowledge and eloquence and discuss this incendiary topic today." I shoot Caitlin a look that, I hope, will tell her that she can't just one-up me so easily. I haven't seen her since yesterday morning and I'm guessing this is her way of spurring me on to make a decision about wanting to go out with her.

While it's mostly all I've been thinking about, I haven't

been able to come up with a good enough reason to do that to myself again. Even though the prospect is tempting, it's the possibly disastrous aftermath I won't be able to cope with—again. "What do you think?" I ask.

"Good one," Nicole shouts and unceremoniously slaps Caitlin on the shoulder.

I repeat the topic and ask them to come up with arguments both supporting and dispelling the theory and then, because Caitlin is in the room, my work is basically done.

I watch her spar with some students and gregariously agree with others and by the time the hour is up, I can only conclude that Caitlin is a natural teacher. She instructs by encouraging questions and by making every single one of the students think for themselves.

When the class finishes, and Nicole and a couple of others are brazen enough to ask Caitlin if she'll join them for a drink, I'm no longer convinced I'll say no if Caitlin asks me to go out with her again. Because, yes, she's beautiful and sexy, but she's also so much more than that. The way she is with the students, and how calmly she spoke to me last night, and her willingness to give me, with all my hang-ups and uncalled-for spur-of-the-moment reactions, another chance, make her so much more than how scrumptious she looks—and how famous she is.

"How about we have a drink after class next week?" Caitlin says to Nicole and the rest. "Because it looks like I'll have to come back if I want the real experience of Miss Greenwood's teaching."

————

"What a cop out," Caitlin says when we're walking to my office. "It was a smart move on your part to have them do a debate, but I really wanted to see you teach."

"Think of the students. They loved it." I stop when we're a few feet away from my office. I'm not even sure why she's following me.

"I meant it when I said I would come back next week."

"I wasn't expecting you today."

"Why not? I said I would come. You gave me explicit permission, remember?"

"Well, yes, but..." *That was before*, I think.

"Besides, I couldn't make it to the Pink Bean this morning and I'm still waiting for an answer to my question." She holds up her hands. "Before you say anything, I wanted to ask if you wanted to go the Pink Bean's open mic night with me tonight. It's the most non-committal date we could possibly go on. It's basically a group activity."

"The open mic?" I had totally forgotten about that.

"Don't worry. I won't pressure you to sing. I've never been to one and I'm just curious."

"I have plans. Er, Eva and I are meant to..." As the words leave my mouth, I'm sure Caitlin can easily tell I'm making them up. Eva will be out—or in—with Declan tonight. I had tentatively said yes to Mona's offer to go for drinks with her and a bunch of other people, but I don't have any firm commitments. "Okay." I haven't been to a Pink Bean open mic night in a while. And it really is more of a group activity. Besides, who am I kidding? After today, I want to spend more time with Caitlin. "I'll be there."

"Any chance of grabbing a bite together first?" Caitlin asks.

"I really can't. I have a lot of work to do before I leave here. The term has only just started and I already have so much paperwork to catch up on."

"I'll see you tonight then." Caitlin lifts two fingers and gives me a quick wave.

CHAPTER EIGHTEEN

It's always strange to be at the Pink Bean when I'm not working. I can't help but look around for cups that need to be cleared and tables that need to be wiped down. It's a reflex after having worked here for two years. Tonight, I'm looking around even more for things out of place, so that I don't feel out of place too much myself.

Kristin is still rounding up open mic participants—one of Robin's colleagues seems very enthusiastic. When I agreed to come, I didn't know that Micky, Robin, Amber and Martha were going to be here as well. I'm not sure Caitlin knew, but she wasn't kidding when she said it would be more of a group activity. While I've been to two dinner parties with these ladies before, things are different now. I've spent time in Caitlin's bed and I'm sure they all know. I'm sure Micky told Robin and Amber—she's not one to keep that sort of information to herself. The only person I trust to not go blabbing about something like this immediately is Amber, who looks a bit uptight herself tonight. Maybe it's Martha's presence.

I remember her invitation for a private yoga lesson which, in my head, only translated into the prospect of more humiliation. If she asks me about it tonight, I'll politely decline.

"What do you mean there's no wine?" Caitlin asks the barista.

"This is a coffee shop," I say. "We don't have a license

to serve alcohol."

"Not every Friday night activity needs to include booze," Amber says.

"Yeah, we have the arts to lift our spirits," Micky says, her tone dripping with irony. I get the distinct impression she didn't really want to be here tonight. Robin probably dragged her here to support her colleague.

"Josephine?" Kristin approaches us. "Are you having a go tonight?"

"What? No." I shake my head.

"My bad. I thought that was why you were here. You don't usually attend so I just assumed."

"Who knows? Maybe some day." Caitlin puts an arm on my shoulder. If this is a date, it's a weird one.

"I don't think so."

"As you wish." Kristin heads to another group of women to rustle up more performers.

I never really understood the allure of the open mic, always considered it a platform for arrogant people desperate to show off a skill they usually don't even master. To be gawked at like that on the carpet that serves as a stage at the Pink Bean. To have a bunch of strangers' eyes on you while you recite poetry that should, in most cases, be kept private.

"I signed up with Kristin earlier," Caitlin says. "I used to dabble in poetry. Why not read some of it here tonight?"

"Someone's missing the spotlight," Sheryl says. "If you miss standing in front of a room of people so much, you're very welcome to teach a course of your choosing. Not many people are offered that much leeway, you know."

"Thanks, but no thanks," Caitlin says.

"The students loved you this afternoon," I say, not letting her get away with turning up like that.

"Looks like this conversation isn't over," Sheryl says and winks at me.

"Please take your seats." Kristin is talking into the mic.

"The fun is about to begin." She glances at the piece of paper in her hands. "First up, we have Meredith, who has become quite the regular. She will be reading from her poetry. Let's give her a big round of applause."

I'm unable to focus much of my attention on Meredith's poem, unlike Caitlin, who seems to be absorbed by it. From the corner of my eye I glance at her. Our chairs are pushed close together and her elbow is only millimeters away from my arm. She is sure to ask me again at the end of this night. Will I say yes?

This isn't really a date, but it feels like a transition between the first one and what could be the actual second one. She's trying so hard for me and I don't know why. Could it be that she actually likes me? I glance at her again. Her dark hair is held together in a ponytail. She's dressed quite casually in jeans but her lips are painted red again, like they were on our date, and a wave of heat swoops through me at the memory of those lips kissing me for the first time.

I want nothing more than to go out with her again, but I'm so scared. Then it comes to me: I'll propose a date. It can even be at her house. But I'll go home after. I won't stay the night. We'll take things slowly. What was I even thinking falling into bed with her so quickly? I was too enthralled by her, too transfixed by the idea of being out with Caitlin. Too fooled by my obvious arousal for her. I won't let that happen again—I won't make the same mistake twice.

Everyone claps, so I follow suit, even though I have no idea what the poem was about. Behind me, Robin whoops. Robin, with the body made entirely out of muscle, or so it seems when she shows up to the Pink Bean in her workout gear.

"Next up, our very own Caitlin James," Kristin announces.

"Go, Caitlin!" Sheryl shouts.

Caitlin briefly puts a hand on my knee—is she nervous? If she is, it's the very first sign I've ever seen of it on her. She rises to her full length and pulls her lips into a wide smile. On the contrary, I guess. She's enjoying every second of this. She must feed off this kind of energy to be able to do the things she does. She's extroversion personified, while me, with my big body and all my angst, I'm the very picture of fear. Of someone who is always waiting for life to get a little bit better before taking a chance.

If I wanted to, I could be on that stage. I let the thought sit in my mind for the briefest of moments, then let it go. Everyone is different. Teaching is enough spotlight for me. If I tried to sing into that microphone, chances are not a single note would make it out of my throat.

I watch Caitlin as she strides to the front.

"Hi everyone," she says with enviable ease. "My name is Caitlin James." A few cheers from the tiny crowd. "And I'm going to read a poem I wrote quite recently, actually." She delves a hand into her jeans pocket and digs up a wrinkled sheet of paper folded into squares. She unfolds it while she holds the crowd's gaze. It reminds me of how she looked at me when she asked me what I liked in bed. It's not just sheer desire I feel when I look back at her now. It's infatuation mixed with respect and, always, unmistakable dread. As though I know in my heart of hearts that this kind of life—the kind of woman Caitlin represents—is not for me.

"It's called 'The Truth'." Caitlin clears her throat and starts reading her poem.

I hang on to her every word. I'm not well-versed in poetry but I'm guessing the most important criteria for it to be good is that it moves the person listening to it, and I am deeply moved. I'm very biased, of course, but I can't help but wonder when she wrote these words.

Her voice is crisp and clear and she reads with a kind bravado that is driving me mad—that is making me want to recant the promise I just made to myself of not sleeping with her again any time soon.

Some people are meant for the stage, I think, as Caitlin ends her poem and I wish she could stay up there a little while longer so I could just look at her, take her in as she makes herself vulnerable, as she gives herself up to the moment like she so easily did when we were in bed together. Is it a learned skill or nature? Maybe a bit of both. I clap my hands together vigorously and she gives us a little bow.

"Thank you," she says, a hand clasped to her chest. "I really appreciate it." She's a woman who knows how to accept applause, who deals with compliments gracefully.

"That was actually quite good." Sheryl pats Caitlin on the shoulder. Robin gives her a wolf whistle as Caitlin sits back down at our table.

"What did you think?" Her eyes seem to search my face for something.

"You're a woman of many talents," I manage to say.

"I thought about letting you read it first," she whispers in my ear, "but the circumstances weren't really right for it."

Kristin calls us to attention again. Someone reads a short story and there are a few more poems and one woman raps while her companion beatboxes and the night passes in a blur of applause and performance. Caitlin's energy radiates onto me and I'm sitting at a table with these wonderful women who are sort of becoming my friends.

"Did Caitlin tell you she's doing my yoga class tomorrow?" Amber says after the performance part of the evening is over. "Only Micky and Robin are not up to it, but Sheryl and Kristin are coming as well. I've even managed to convince Martha to join."

"That's great."

"How about you, Josephine?" Amber asks.

"Oh, I don't think so."

"Maybe you could stop by some time next week? For that private lesson?"

"I'll think about it."

We are joined by Martha, who puts a hand on Amber's

shoulder. "You can't convert all of us," she says. "It's just not statistically possible."

"Doesn't mean I can't try." Amber gives Martha a warm smile.

"You *are* pretty hard to resist." Martha leans into her a little. "At least for me."

I'm quickly beginning to feel like a fifth wheel. They must have taken their relationship to the next level. So this is what that looks like. I'm sure they're both seeing stars when they go to bed together. They seem to glow in each other's company. They look like a couple that makes perfect sense.

"I'm dying for a glass of wine." Caitlin has walked up to us. "Who's up for it?"

"I'm teaching tomorrow morning," Amber says.

"I'm with her," Martha adds.

"Micky? Robin? How about you?"

"We have the kids and, er, kind of a big weekend planned."

I've been so caught up in my own frustrations that I forgot Micky was going to ask Robin to move in with her. Is she alluding to that? If she is, I'm sure I'll hear all about it on Monday.

"Come on up to ours," Sheryl says. "I'll pour you a nice glass while Kristin finishes up here."

"Oh, no. That's all right," Caitlin says, her lips stiffening a bit. "You don't have to do that."

"How many times do we need to have this conversation? Yes, I'm a recovering alcoholic, but yes, we still have wine in the fridge for Kristin and our guests. Come on, Kristin will be happy to have someone to share a bottle with in the comfort of her own home." She looks at me. "Are you coming up, Josephine?"

"I would love to, but I really can't." How many times have I said no to people tonight? I'm beginning to notice it a bit too much. "I have a lot of work to do tomorrow." I give an apologetic shrug, expecting Sheryl will understand.

"You work this girl too hard, Sheryl," Caitlin says. She glances at Sheryl, and takes a step in my direction. "Give me a minute. I'll be right up."

She takes me aside, her hands lingering near mine. "Can I see you this weekend?"

"Er, yes." Butterflies storm my belly as she looks into my eyes. "Sunday?"

"Your place?" She sends me a crooked smile.

"Why not?" I laugh at her persistence. "Come for lunch?"

"I look forward to it already." Her fingers brush against mine as she presses a hot kiss to my cheek.

———

After I get home and find the apartment empty, I pour myself a glass of wine and retreat to my room. When I put down the glass on my nightstand and my eye falls on the drawer where I keep a very small collection of sex toys, I get a tingle in my belly. I remember Caitlin's fingers briefly intertwining with mine. The imprint of her lips on my cheek. I bring my hand to my cheek, as if wanting to catch whatever is left of her kiss—capturing the memory of it.

All her actions toward me are so sensual, so full of her desire for me. And tonight, after seeing her read that poem out loud, I don't want to analyze whether I'm worthy of Caitlin's affections. I want to do something else with my thoughts of her. I couldn't get her off my mind even if I wanted to. Her presence is here with me, in my room, where she has never set foot. When I close my eyes, I can remember the smell of her perfume. I can see her looking at me. I can see her talking into the mic with a confidence that not only astounds me, but greatly arouses me as well.

I open the drawer and take out my 'neck massager', which I've only tried on my actual neck once, but has a much more relaxing effect when used elsewhere. I can only use this particular object when I'm home alone because the noise it produces makes me feel too self-conscious. Eva would put two and two together quickly if she heard its distinct hum from my room in the middle of the night.

She and Declan might be coming home soon. I have no idea. All I know is that I'm in a rush, which adds to my arousal.

I take a sip of wine, plug in the appliance and lay it on my bed, ready to go. I slip out of my jeans and panties quickly, already imagining it's Caitlin taking them off. The effect is instant.

I spread my legs wide and I don't have to try very hard to conjure up Caitlin between them. She has spent time there after all. I switch on the vibrator and the whirring sound, the prospect it promises, intensifies the tingle in my belly. I want her so much, yet there's so much standing between us. All the things in my head, all my fears and doubts and body issues. None of them will bother me now. Because it's just me and my trusted machine. I bring the head between my legs and then it's all Caitlin in my mind again.

It's so easy to come like this. It's a matter of mere minutes. As the vibrator buzzes against my clit, I imagine my finger slipping inside of Caitlin again. I remember her reaction, how she begged me. Then I imagine her finger doing the same to me. Two. Three. Caitlin spreading me wide. And I come hard, every cell of me filled to the brim with thoughts of Caitlin. My body convulses, my legs twitch and I all but cry out her name.

CHAPTER NINETEEN

When I open the door Caitlin's face is hidden behind a bunch of flowers. She drops them to her belly and gives me a wide smile.

"I brought a bottle of wine as well." She holds it up. "Didn't know which one you would prefer."

I usher her in, accepting both gifts with a funny feeling in my tummy. Will I be able to stand my ground and keep this from going too fast again? When I kiss her on the cheek, she turns her face so that I almost kiss her on the lips. To me, it might feel like starting over, but maybe to her it just feels like moving things swiftly along.

I show her the living room which is the size of her hallway.

"Exactly how I had imagined it," she says. She's wearing jeans and a button-down shirt and even though her outfit is quite casual, she still looks too glamorous for this apartment.

"Trip down memory lane?" We both sit down in the sofa that has become Eva and Declan's terrain of late. When I told Eva who was coming over, she got so excited it was difficult to get her to stick to her promise of giving me the place to myself for a couple of hours like every Sunday.

"It seems like a lifetime ago." Caitlin sits close to me, our knees almost touching.

"Are you hungry?" I ask. "I made a salad."

"Where do you eat?" She looks around. We don't have

room for a dining table in the lounge.

"Often in front of the television," I confess. "But we do have a small table in the kitchen."

"For some reason, being here makes me feel so… advanced in age."

"You insisted on coming here."

"I did." She lets her glance wander around. "I wanted to see how you live. See your things. Your books. Your room."

"All in good time." I push myself up. Knowing this couch very well, I know how to rise from it semi-gracefully. "Let's eat and drink first."

Caitlin follows me into the kitchen, which might actually be the nicest place in the entire apartment. The landlord had a cheap but brand new kitchen installed before Eva and I moved in and we've managed to keep it in pretty pristine condition.

There's a small table with three chairs around it by the window. The view is a bunch of rooftops, which is better than a brick wall. I often sit at this table to work, staring out of the window when taking a break, waiting for the occasional bird to fly by. Never in my wildest dreams had I imagined I'd one day be sitting here with Caitlin James.

I pour us some drinks, serve the salad and slice some bread. Then I sit gazing at Caitlin's face. There's a silence I don't immediately know how to fill. All I hear is the clatter of cutlery against plates, then we both start to say something at the same time.

"I'm sure what you were about to say is much more interesting." I raise a suggestive eyebrow.

"You assume too much." She puts her fork down. "Thanks for inviting me here and thanks for lunch." She takes a sip of water. "Is this a date, then?"

"I don't see how it could not be."

She picks up her fork again. "Good. I was hoping you would see it that way."

"I really liked that poem you read on Friday. It was very…" I pause to look for the right word. "Emotional."

"You think so? I wrote it after things fell apart with Michelle. I was feeling pretty emotional at the time."

"Have you written many?" We've finished lunch and are lounging at the kitchen table.

"Not really. Only when the muse strikes me. She tends to only visit me when I'm down in the dumps."

After Caitlin told me about Michelle, I googled various combinations of their names together, but I didn't find any mention of them on the internet.

"So the less poetry you write, the better your life is going?"

"If you put it that way." She slants her head.

"What was she like? Michelle?"

Caitlin purses her lips together. "Pretty formidable. Impossible to ignore. Typical New York loudmouth."

My curiosity is peaked. If only I could get her last name. It would make the googling so much easier.

"I don't really want to talk about Michelle. I was sad when it ended and it definitely contributed to my decision to move back to Australia, but these things happen. Our arrangement didn't suit her anymore and there's only so much talking you can do about things like that. Moreover, I didn't want to be with someone who I had to convince over and over again to be with me—all of me."

"You mean have an open relationship with you?"

"Open. Non-monogamous. Certainly non-traditional. Call it what you will." She takes a sip of the wine I poured earlier. "Monogamy works for very few people. It's a fact that's clear as day. Yet so many people resist it."

"Is it really, though?" I can think of plenty of examples of monogamous relationships that seem to work perfectly fine.

"I don't want to paint the wrong picture here. We

weren't sleeping with other people every other week. We had very clear rules."

"I'm quite curious about the rules."

"They tend to change organically over time and I don't believe there should be too many." Caitlin goes into the charismatic teacher mode I saw her deploy when she guest lectured at the university. "Basically, it's just a matter of respect for your partner. I would never trade time with her for time with anyone else. And because we lived in different cities, we had the rule of never being with anyone else when we were in the same city. It was all pretty straightforward."

"Hm." I nod.

"What's your position on the subject?" She brings her elbows to the table and leans over.

I was afraid this question would come up sooner rather than later. "My relationship track record hasn't really given me much cause to contemplate the matter."

"You're an academic. Surely you can theorize."

"I distinctly remember having a conversation about non-monogamous relationships a few months ago with Sheryl. She claimed that when she was doing her PhD she knew quite a few people who very strongly believed in keeping relationships wide open but that she had the impression that in the past decade especially, young people hanker more for a traditional relationship."

"I know very well how Sheryl feels about open relationships. I'm more curious about how you feel about them."

"I'm not sure. I mean, er, I'm really not someone who's into one-night stands. I much prefer to know the person I'm about to go to bed with."

"So I gathered." Her smile is sweet. "But what if that changed?"

"What do you mean?"

"What if you were perfectly capable of having very satisfying sex with a woman you'd just met and are very attracted to?"

I huff out a breath. It only takes a split second for my cheeks to burn bright red. "Ouch," I say.

"Oh, no. I really didn't mean it like that. That came out wrong."

"Tell me honestly, Caitlin. Do you see me as a younger, less evolved version of yourself?"

"What? No." She pushes her chair back. "Where did you get that?"

"You're asking me to 'theorize'"—I curl my fingers into air quotes—"about open relationships, while you know very well that I..." I can't say it.

"Hey." She crouches next to me. "Open relationships do not equal orgasms with strangers."

I snort. "Maybe we should save this particular topic for later."

"Okay." Her fingertips press into my jeans. "How about you show me the rest of your apartment?"

"Okay." I'm pretty sure she means my bedroom, which I have tidied, but have no intention of spending time in with her. Not today.

As I get up, she slips her hand in mine, and I show her the tiny bathroom, which now has a third cup with a toothbrush on the side of the sink. Then we stand outside of my bedroom door.

"That's Eva's room and here is my kingdom." I show her in. For an instant, it feels like that time she ended up in my office. Like there's not enough air in the room for both of us.

"These look familiar." She walks over to my bookcase, the shelves of which are sagging under the weight I make them carry. "You haven't sold them on eBay yet." She taps the stack of books she signed for me.

"Haven't been that strapped for cash just yet."

She chuckles. "I've been meaning to talk to you about possibly using some of your research for one of my books.

Or one of our books, if you like. But I always get so distracted when I'm with you." Caitlin crashes down onto my bed. I lean my hip awkwardly against my desk. "This hardly seems like the right environment to discuss it either." She shoots me a smile then looks around some more. She picks up the book I have on my nightstand, twirls it around in her hands and reads the title out loud. "*Don't Wait Until Tomorrow For What You Can Achieve Today*. Is it any good?"

Good? How can I explain to her that what makes a book like that *good* for me is not what will make it a must-read for her without sounding too defensive?

"You can borrow it once I've finished it."

"Thanks and I don't intend to." She puts the book back and leans back on her palms. "Wait until tomorrow, I mean." She smiles up at me. How did she end up on my bed so quickly? "Come sit with me?"

"I—I would feel more comfortable in the living room."

"Oh." A flash of disappointment crosses her face. "Sure." She pushes herself up with enviable elegance. "Hey." She takes my hand and pulls me to her. "I wasn't being presumptuous. I promise."

I'm so close I can smell her perfume again—a scent that's difficult to forget. Deep inside of me, something unclenches, but I know I have to be strong. This moment may feel promising, but nothing has changed—though I'm not entirely sure yet how to go about changing the things I would need to in order to successfully sleep with Caitlin.

"Can I kiss you?" she asks.

"Yes. In the living room," I say coyly.

———

Caitlin is straddling me in the sofa. Clearly me not wanting to stay in the bedroom has had no effect on her desire to kiss me again and again. My thighs are pressed together between her hips and her chest pushes into mine every time she leans in for another round. She tastes of cool wine and the tangy dressing I made and her hands are in my hair again and she's slowly driving me crazy.

"As much as I would like to," I try to say in between another onslaught of kisses. My voice is breathless and unconvincing.

"What, Josephine? Are you going to ask me to leave now?" She smiles a wicked smile, then bites softly into my earlobe. "Because I would very much like to stay a little longer."

"Please, can I, er, just ask you a question."

"Shoot," she whispers in my ear, prolonging the word, her breath tickling my skin.

"You can't kiss me while I'm asking it." I push her away a bit, which is hard to do while I'm totally enveloped by her.

She leans back, her behind on my knees.

"It's just hard for me to wrap my head around all of this. It's clear as day why I like you. You're one of my idols. I have so much respect for your work. You are one of the sexiest women I've ever met. It's no wonder I'm infatuated with you. It would, in fact, be strange if I wasn't. But you? You keep coming back? Is it because you want to question me about my dissertation research? And if so, why haven't you done so already?"

"Wow," Caitlin says on a sigh. "Way to kill the mood." She narrows her eyes. "Are you really that insecure that you have to explicitly ask me what I see in you?"

"Ouch again." I look away.

"You can't ask me a question like that, have me counter with a perfectly understandable follow-up question and then act all wounded."

"I wish I could be more like you. Confident and ready to lose myself in a bout of enjoyable sex at the drop of a hat. Carefree and flirting and sharing my visions on open relationships. But I'm not that girl. I have so many questions running through my head every time we are together. And I do want to spend time with you. God, it's all I want, but I just fail to see what you could possibly be getting out of this."

She brings a finger to my chin and slowly turns my head so I face her again. "I don't want you to be any other girl than yourself, Josephine. And I see the terror show up in your eyes. But... I happen to think you are beautiful and interesting and very smart, except, perhaps, when it comes to dealing with people who have a, and I'd like to stress the following word, *mutual* crush on you." She plants her hands on my shoulders. "I know you're scared of going to bed with me again. Perhaps you even think I'm somehow disappointed in you, even though I've already told you that what happened was totally normal. Just as I know that, if only you could not be so afraid all the time—afraid of what I or other people might think of you—you would be more than smart enough to see this exactly for what it is. It's two people liking each other and getting to know each other better. Maybe even the beginning of something wonderful, if you don't overthink it to death." She scoots her knees a little closer. "At one point, you are going to have to get out of your head. There are no two ways about it. I'd like to be there when that happens."

"I keep fucking up. I'm sorry."

Caitlin shakes her head. "And you keep apologizing for just being you."

I swallow the next *I'm sorry* that sits at the tip of my tongue.

"Tell you what." She kisses me on the cheek, her lips barely making contact. "With your permission, I would like to kiss you some more." Again, a touch of the lips barely perceptible. "And we'll take things slowly. That's perfectly fine by me. As long as we go on another date next week."

"Sounds pretty good to me." I pull her close by the back of the head and kiss her fully on the lips.

CHAPTER TWENTY

"So?" I ask Micky first thing when I see her on Monday morning. "Did you talk to your kids?"

"I talked to my kids, to their father *and* to Robin," she says while arranging the chairs around the tables. "Darren could hardly object, seeing as, according to Christopher and Olivia, Lisa is basically already living with him. And everyone said yes. Robin is pretty easy to like, I guess." She stops what she's doing and walks over to me. "My house is quite small, but it'll be cozy." She sends me a wide smile. "It feels so… I don't know, incredibly warm in my heart, no matter how corny that may sound, to make plans to live with someone again. I mean, she's not going to move in tomorrow, but the ground work has been done. The kids are okay with it. Now I just have to tell my mother that her daughter will be shacking up with a woman."

"I'm really happy for you Micky. That's amazing news."

"And how was your weekend, Jo?" She bats her eyelashes. "I saw you sitting terribly close to a certain Miss Caitlin James last Friday. Are things back on track?"

I remember the state Caitlin left me in last night. When she left, for a split second, I could barely stop myself from asking whether I could go back home with her. But then Eva and Declan came home and I could focus all my energy on driving Eva crazy with tales of how utterly amazing Caitlin is.

"She came over for lunch yesterday. It was fun."

"And they say you should never meet your heroes. Good for you."

"I know." I glow a little on the inside as I head to the door. "Time to open up."

"Do you want to have lunch with me and Amber later?"

"Depends. How many times is she going to ask me to do yoga this time?"

"Just ignore her."

"She seemed pretty close to Martha last Friday. How's that progressing?"

The door opens, announcing our first customer of the day.

"Come to lunch and you can ask her all about it yourself."

"It will be my pleasure," I say, and shoot the customer a wide smile.

———

"Hi, Josephine. How are you?" Zoya asks while waggling her eyebrows suggestively. I wonder exactly how close she and Caitlin are.

"I'm very well, thanks," I say matter-of-factly. "In the neighborhood again?"

"Caitlin keeps raving about how much she enjoys living here. I've had some upheaval in my life recently so I thought I'd spend some more time here. The coffee shops are not too bad." She looks at the table were Caitlin usually sits. "Is Caitlin coming today?"

I should know more about Caitlin's whereabouts than her now? "I think so."

"Don't you just love that penthouse she has?" She whistles through her teeth. "I wouldn't mind living there. I'll tell you that."

I hand her her vanilla soy latte. "It's very nice."

"Zoya Das?" Someone has approached the counter. "I'm such a big fan."

Zoya turns to the woman and gives her a big smile. Zoya has the kind of television show that would surely get her recognized, but only by a certain kind of, more mature, crowd. People my age don't have the patience to watch the sort of in-depth interviews Zoya specializes in. We'd much rather watch two-minute YouTube clips of Ellen Degeneres dancing.

"What's with all these famous people turning up here all of a sudden?" Micky asks. "We'll be in paparazzi shots next, you and me, Jo."

"It only takes one to attract many." I look at Zoya who is walking toward a table with the woman.

"But Caitlin isn't even that famous. I didn't know her," Micky teases.

"But now we have Zoya as a regular Pink Bean customer as well."

"What do you make of her?" Micky asks. "I like her but I don't know what her intentions are. She's hard to read."

"She went through a pretty bad break-up not long ago. I guess she's just trying to find her feet again."

Just then, Caitlin walks in, rescuing Zoya from her fan.

She gives me a warm smile before ordering, but I beat her to it and say, "A flat white coming right up, Miss James."

"Do you have time to sit with us? I didn't even know Zoya was going to be here."

"I believe she has her eye on your penthouse."

"Does she now?" Caitlin shoots me a wink. "We're still on for Wednesday?"

I've already given her the coffee, but she lingers by the counter.

"Oh, yes."

"Can't wait." She leans over the counter and whispers. "Is it really bad form to kiss the barista?"

I chuckle. "You're Caitlin James. You can get away with it."

She gives me a light peck on the cheek and joins Zoya.

"Wednesday, huh?" Micky says as soon as Caitlin is out of earshot.

"Good to know nothing gets past you."

"I wasn't intentionally eavesdropping. I just work here, too." She has a smug smile plastered across her face.

———

"Jo was asking about a progress update on you and Martha earlier." Micky drops me right in it.

"And I'm sure you're in no way curious yourself," Amber replies.

We're having lunch at Micky's. Between her house, Sheryl and Kristin's apartment and Caitlin's penthouse, my real estate aspirations for when I, somehow, someday, start earning some actual money, have certainly gone up.

"Martha doesn't come to the Pink Bean that often so we can't follow along with the action."

"She's a busy woman. Full time job. Three children. Two grandkids."

"A burgeoning love affair?" Micky asks.

"I guess we have taken things to the next level." Amber sits there glowing.

Micky slams her palm on the table. "Now you tell me? When did this happen?"

"I don't have to tell you every detail of what's going on between me and Martha." Amber pricks a piece of tomato onto her fork.

"Of course you do. I'm your best friend. I tell *you* everything."

Amber chuckles, then turns to me. "Don't you agree that Micky has become insufferable now that she's about to shack up with a posh banker?"

"Totally."

"Don't let Amber lure you into changing the subject. I can see right through that," Micky says.

"Okay. Fine." Amber puts down her fork and smiles triumphantly. "We slept together this weekend. It was amazing."

"Hallelujah!" Micky exclaims.

"I'm not giving you any more details than that."

"That information will last me a while." Micky's tone has softened. "I'm just happy for you, Amber. That it's becoming something real." She turns to me. "Do you know the story? Martha was meant for me. I had a dinner party at this very table and Amber snatched her up right from under my nose."

Amber rolls her eyes. "It wasn't like that at all."

I giggle. Being around Micky and Amber makes me feel a little giddy. Although there are some things I would like to ask Amber, in private. Maybe I should take her up on her offer of a private yoga lesson. I could ask her in confidence how she experienced sex with a new person for the first time. Maybe I could even get her opinion on open relationships while I'm at it.

I tune out their banter for an instant, remembering how Caitlin kissed me on the cheek earlier. How she made me feel so special and wanted again. Already, a bout of nerves tears through me when I think of our next date. If only I could emerge from it looking as satisfied and pleased with myself as Amber.

"Don't let Caitlin pressure you into doing anything you don't want to, Josephine. Okay?" Amber says.

"I think Josephine can take care of herself," Micky says.

"I haven't talked to her yet about our dalliance two years ago. After this weekend, it doesn't seem so important anymore." Amber draws her lips into another wide smile. "I'm sure Caitlin has forgotten all about it, anyway."

"The topic hasn't really come up," I say.

"They have far more interesting things to discuss than you, Amber," Micky says.

"I'm sure you do." Amber winks at me. I wish I could have only a fraction of her calm demeanor. Yoga is beginning to sound more and more enticing.

CHAPTER TWENTY-ONE

When I arrive at Caitlin's for our date, I have brought my running gear and a set of clothes I feel comfortable working in the next day. I leave the bag in my car to not come over too presumptuous. After all, I'm the one who wants to take things slowly.

As I walk in, I'm baffled again by the elegance of the place. And how effortlessly Caitlin fits into it. We drink champagne on the balcony overlooking the city.

"I would like to request an official meeting with you," she says. "I don't want to talk shop with you tonight, but can I come by your office some time this week to talk about my book? If you have the time, of course. I'm putting together a proposal and I would like to add some topics you know much more about than I do."

"We can talk about it now."

Caitlin shakes her head. "No. Not tonight. I have other plans for us tonight."

"Do you?" I look into her dark eyes. Her lips are painted a shade darker than the usual bright red.

Caitlin stares into my eyes and nods. "I have ordered food, by the way. It should be here soon."

I look away from her and gaze at the view. A beat passes in silence while I brace myself for what I'm about to say next.

"I've been thinking about what you asked me this weekend. My position on open relationships? It's pretty clear

I don't have a position on it. Not yet. But it made me wonder about something." I shuffle in my seat and take another sip of my drink.

"Yes?"

"We've established that we're dating and that, um, we like each other."

"We have indeed." Caitlin has a crooked smile on her face, as though she knows exactly what I'm about to ask her.

"While all of this is happening, are you seeing other people?"

Caitlin raises her eyebrows. "And when you say *seeing* you actually mean *sleeping with*?"

I shrug. My heart is beating very fast. This was definitely something I wanted to discuss tonight, but the champagne on an empty stomach has made me a little overzealous.

"No, Josephine, of course I'm not sleeping with anyone else." She huffs out a breath. "I thought my intentions were clear."

"They are, but all that talk of open relationships. It made me wonder." My shoulders relax a little.

"It would be very disrespectful of me to be sleeping with someone else while I'm courting you. Don't you think?"

I nod. "It would." I sit up a bit straighter. "I get your point," I say, "I just had to ask."

The intercom buzzes. Caitlin jumps up. "That'll be the food. I'll be right back."

While she saunters inside, I can't help but wonder if, when it comes to it, I would even want an open relationship. Whether it would be a price I'd have no choice to pay to be with her. But my mind can't even properly go there yet. Perhaps it's denial. Or more fear. But right now, what Caitlin and I are doing, is about something else entirely than me finding out if I'm up for an open relationship.

"Here we are." She plants a huge pizza box on the table. "One large pepperoni."

———

"Life is complicated. Any age you're at, there's shit to deal with and un-fairytale-like hurdles to cross. But," Caitlin holds up her glass, "it does get easier when you get older. To put it very simply: you start caring less about non-important stuff and the important things get easier because you've had time to figure out what it is that they are."

I've eaten two slices of pizza and am staring out into the night. We've almost finished the bottle of champagne. "What *is* important to you at this stage of your life?" I ask.

"I just want to do things that make a difference and that make me happy. Not everything I do has to meet both criteria. I'm not that unrealistic. But that's another reason I came back. Being an academic wasn't making me very happy anymore. I was feeling more and more constricted. That's why Sheryl can nag me all she wants, but I won't be taking a position at the University of Sydney. I want to write instead, and talk about what I've learned." She puts her glass down. "And do I think it's fair that just because my old mug was allowed on television on a regular basis I can afford to choose what to do these days?" She shakes her head. "TV is definitely an overvalued and overpaid medium, but it is effective in getting certain points across." She looks at me. "Am I babbling?"

"No." I think every single word she says is interesting. "Go on."

"The fact is that I will take the job at ANBC just so I can afford to do other things that are more important to me. Like this book we'll be talking about soon." She shoots me a smile.

I've had too much champagne to experience stress in response to the look she just sent me. She stretches out her arm. I do the same with mine and interlace our fingers.

"I'd like to ask if you want to stay the night. It doesn't mean we can't take it slow. We don't have to go any further than some kissing"—a chuckle—"and perhaps some heavy petting. You set the boundaries."

"I have all my stuff in the car."

Caitlin laughs. "Does that mean yes?"

"As long as you won't keep me from going for a run before I start work tomorrow morning." Her hand feels soft in mine.

"I wouldn't dream of it."

"Then I don't see why not." A slew of butterflies takes flight in my stomach.

"I'm glad."

"Have you always lived alone?" I ask, suddenly curious.

"Mostly yes, but not always." She gently scratches my palm with a fingernail. "Have you ever lived alone? Or always with friends?"

"I could never afford to live on my own. I like having someone around. What Eva and I have going is good, although I suspect that might change soon. She and Declan have been together for a while. Much longer than Micky and Robin, for instance, and they're already moving in together."

"You think your roommate is going to desert you?"

"It would only be natural for her and her boyfriend to move in together."

"Then you'll have to find another roomie."

"I know." Caitlin's fingernails are distracting me. "She's also my best friend. I would miss having her around so much."

"Declan could move in with you two? Isn't he there already most of the time?"

"You've seen our flat. It does not have space for a bloke."

"Fair enough." She tugs at my hand. "Do you want to go inside?"

I know very well what that means.

"Sure." At least it will keep me from worrying about my living situation for a while. Either way, our lease isn't up until the end of the term.

"Come on," Caitlin says.

———

We've moved from the balcony to the sofa to Caitlin's bedroom pretty swiftly. She's all over me again and not giving any indication of stopping what we're doing any time soon.

At least we're still fully clothed, lying on top of the covers. And I feel the fire burning inside of me, just as I did last time I was here, but not that much has changed since then.

Caitlin must feel my hesitance because she pauses to scan my face. "Can I ask you a question?" she asks.

"Of course." Her hair is all over the place and her lipstick is smudged but not in a comical way. Caitlin always looks sexy to me.

"Do you masturbate?"

My eyes go wide.

"I'm asking for a reason." Her finger skates along the bare skin of my upper arm.

"I do."

"So you have the physical ability to reach orgasm."

It doesn't sound like a question, but I nod anyway.

"Will you show me?" she asks, her finger dipping down to my collarbone, tracing a line there.

"Show you? How I masturbate?" Something coils in my stomach.

"I'll help you," she says.

"I—I'm not sure if I can." The top button of her blouse has already come undone.

"How about I show you first? You watch while I get myself off. Does that sound like a fair trade?"

"In theory, it sounds perfectly plausible, but as I said, I'm not sure I can."

"Don't question whether you can or can't. Just watch me. Okay?" She sinks her teeth into her bottom lip.

"It's worth a try." Definitely if I get to see her touch

herself first.

"All right." She shuffles close again. "I'm pretty hot and bothered already." Her lips draw into a smile before she kisses me again.

When our tongues meet, most of my nerves are pushed down by the sheer excitement of being allowed to watch her, no matter the tradeoff afterwards.

We undress each other until I'm in my underwear and Caitlin is completely naked. "Ready for the show?" she asks, the huskiness in her voice a clear indicator that she's thoroughly enjoying this.

I nod. "Where do you want me?"

"I want you to watch me. *All of me.*"

I crawl to the end of the bed, feeling very much like the voyeur she has made of me. A pulse picks up speed between my legs. This might be the most arousing sight I've ever laid eyes on. Caitlin spreads her legs wide for me to see it all. She's making a show of it. Running her fingers along her chest, back up again, circling her nipples.

Her head is propped up on a pillow and she makes eye contact, but my gaze is drawn elsewhere. Who knew this could be so thrilling?

She brings both her hands between her wide-spread legs. One rests on her inner thigh, the index finger of the other skates along her pussy lips. She repeats the motion a few times and as much as I wish it was my tongue following the length of her lips, I'm enjoying this show very much. So much so, that I feel an animal impulse to plunge my hand into my panties and go on this journey with her. I resist, for now.

Caitlin dips her fingertip between her lips and only then can I see how wet she is. Her finger comes away coated in juice. With her other hand she spreads her lips while her wet finger starts circling her clit. She gives a little moan and I have to look at her face. She's still looking at me from under hooded lids. I can see she's totally lost in the moment. That she was easily able to achieve complete surrender again.

Then I can't stop myself anymore. I don't plunge my hand all the way into my panties, instead I draw a circle over the fabric, trying to soothe my own throbbing clit, the same way she is doing.

Caitlin must see me doing this. She intensifies the speed of her finger, stimulating her clit, baring herself to me completely. As I sit there, I realize that making someone come and watching them do it to themselves are two entirely different things. This time around, I get to see every change in her face, I get to see her muscles flex as she inches closer. I get to see it all.

When she comes, her head thrown back and her toes all curled up, I'm ready to tear off my underwear and throw myself onto her.

"That was so hot," I whisper in her ear, no longer able to stay away from her warm body.

"Yeah?" She turns onto her side and brings her finger to my lips. I can smell her and it arouses me even more. I take her hand and suck the juices off her finger the way she did with mine last week. "I saw you touching yourself." Her voice is still just a whisper. "It was quite helpful." She snickers.

I don't say anything, just suck her finger deep into my mouth. I'm so aroused, but I know it's not my level of arousal that's the problem. It's letting go in front of someone else. Getting over myself, and what I believe my body makes other people feel, and just do it. The way I do when it's just me in my room.

"My turn," I say, after letting go of her finger.

"Do you want me to do anything?" she asks.

I shake my head.

"But it's okay if I watch? The way you did?"

"Yes." Just saying the word carries its own excitement. I'm not sure how this is going to go, but I have to try. I want to.

"Let me help you with these." She unclasps my bra. Kisses me on the lips for a long time, before hooking her thumbs under the waistband of my drenched panties.

Then, there I lie. Caitlin shuffles back onto the bed. She has a soft smile on her face, but I think it better not to focus too much on her face, no matter how gorgeous it is. This isn't about Caitlin. This is about me overcoming something. Why have I never thought of this before with my previous girlfriends? I was probably too mortified to even consider it.

I spread my legs and close my eyes. I pretend I'm in my room but it's as if I can feel Caitlin's gaze on me. It strangely spurs me on. I conjure up images from minutes ago. Caitlin doing to her body what I'm doing to mine now. It makes me feel like it's her hands on my body, yet I know, in the back of my brain, like a sort of safety net, that they are mine. This is me. Only me. She's watching but that's it. I'm in charge. In control.

I think of her head falling back when she came. And how she smiled at me so sweetly. How she now has the habit of slipping to the side of the counter at the Pink Bean and sneaking me a kiss. And how it was Caitlin's gentle insistence that got me here, circling my clit before her very eyes. I'm sufficiently warmed up. If it was just me, I probably would have sealed the deal already. But I'm in Caitlin's penthouse, in her swanky bed, my hands busy between my legs.

The situation isn't entirely different but enough for me to get out of my head. No one else is doing this to me, is demanding something of me that I can't give. For a brief moment, as my finger keeps touching my clit in the exact way I know will get me off, I consider opening my eyes and re-confirming my surroundings, but I don't. I fear it may be a step too far and why ruin it now, when I've already come this far?

Of course, I know that Caitlin is watching, that her eyes are all over this body of mine, but what was it that she said last time? We are all responsible for our own orgasms. If that's the case, and I believe it is, I'm taking responsibility tonight.

Yes, this is the same body as last week, but it's also the same body she was all over earlier. It's the body attached to the person, the me she has shown such kindness to. It's my body and perhaps I will never be able to be proud of it, but I know what it can do. It can have an orgasm right about now.

I screw my eyes a little tighter, block out everything else and, in a moment of extreme irony, think of Caitlin spreading her legs, while she's sitting right next to me, just to push me over the edge. Because I'm touching myself, and I'm me, the image in my head has more power than the actual person on the bed with me.

Her smile. Her lips. Her hands. Her fingers. Her naked body. Her wide-spread legs. They are a montage in my mind, on repeat, flickering from one image to the other, until they blend into a crash of white as warmth spreads to my muscles and my pussy contracts around nothing. As the last spasm rips through me, I open my eyes. Caitlin's gaze on me is intense, unmistakable.

"Christ," she mutters, and crawls up, throwing an arm around me. "I think I'm ready to go again," she whispers in my ear. "You looked so incredibly sexy."

"I must have made a silly orgasm face," I joke.

"No." I can feel her shaking her head against my cheek. "There was absolutely nothing silly about that."

An unfamiliar lightness settles within me. I just had my very first orgasm with another person in the room. Things are looking up. I turn on my side to better look her in the wide, brown eyes.

"Thank you for suggesting this."

"Thank you for trusting me." She leans in to kiss me. "It's a big deal."

I sink into her embrace, a new-found sense of contentment swirling through me. And this is only the beginning of this journey we're on, I think, as our bodies come together, her breasts pressing into mine. I can't wait for what's next.

CHAPTER TWENTY-TWO

"Don't you have to go for a run?" Caitlin asks. I've just woken up and I couldn't feel more different this morning than when I last woke up in her bed.

"Yes." I snuggle up to her, putting my head on her shoulder.

"Then what are you waiting for?" She pulls me closer, her hand pressing against my back.

"It's hard to say." I press a kiss to the warm spot of skin my mouth is closest to. Waking up like this feels like a dream. "What time is it?"

"6:48 to be exact."

"I don't have to commute so I have some time."

"Are you the same person as last night? The one who claimed to have brought her running shoes and who should, under no circumstances, be kept from her daily run?"

"I usually don't wake up with the esteemed Professor James in my bed." I throw a leg over hers. "Kind of makes me feel like I'm chained to it."

"You're calling me your ball and chain already?" Caitlin kisses me on the crown of my head.

"I don't know how else to explain it. Even if the place were on fire, I'm still not sure I could tear myself away from you to bring myself to safety."

"Now you're just being dramatic." Caitlin slips from under me and turns on her side. "Did you sleep well?"

"Like a log. You?" I kiss her on the nose, before

starting to push myself up.

She nods.

"I need to call my sister in five minutes. If only you were more famous and she knew who you were, I could put us on speaker to impress her."

"I'm so very sorry about that." She grins.

"I need to find my phone first." Calling Bea is such an ingrained part of my routine, I always keep my phone next to my bed. But nothing is normal this morning.

"Here's an idea." Caitlin pulls me to her again. "After your call, join me in the shower. I'll be waiting. All soaped up."

"Best get it done then." I fling the covers off and, not bothering to wrap myself in a sheet this time, tip-toe to the bathroom.

––––––––

Caitlin is soaping my back in the most distracting manner. "Do you sing in the shower?" she asks.

"Sometimes." I hold my head away from the spray of water to hear her better.

"What's in your shower repertoire?"

I turn around, our bodies skimming against each other. "What's in yours?" I counter.

"I quite like some Lionel Richie to get me going in the morning. Some 'Dancing on the Ceiling'. That kind of thing."

"Are you going to give me a taste?"

She raises her eyebrows. "I'm not sure you're ready for that kind of performance."

"I've seen you read poetry. That was foreplay enough."

"You asked for it." Her foamy hands slither up my arms. She clears her throat and grabs me by the shoulders, takes a deep breath. After she has sung one line at the top of her lungs, I have to pull my head as far away as possible from this source of aural terror.

"You're doing that on purpose," I shout over her.

"That can't really be anyone's singing voice."

She keeps holding me by the arms. "You asked for it. Now you're going to enjoy it." She sings some more and it sounds even worse than before, like a hundred kittens crying in the back of her throat.

"That was a truly horrendous experience," I say when she finishes.

"You still want to go out with me?" She stands there all wet and giggly.

"I'm not sure. This has kind of burst my Caitlin James bubble," I joke.

"You show me how it's done then." She sucks her bottom lip into her mouth.

"This is how you trick me into singing for you?"

"You have no choice. You have to cleanse the air by singing another song. The ghost of my horrific singing will linger in this shower forever if you don't. You must chase it away." She splashes some water in my direction. "See, it's already starting to act up. Do something." She presses me against the wall. "It's coming for you first."

Caitlin is irresistible. I'd sing for her out of pure joy alone. "Okay." I take a breath and launch into "I Will Always Love You", the Whitney Houston version.

Caitlin takes a step back and clasps a hand to her mouth.

I finish after the first chorus, having belted it out much more than I usually would.

"Either the water's getting cold or you just gave me goosebumps," Caitlin says.

"Has the ghost fled?"

"What?" She gives me a funny look.

"The ghost of your dreadful singing?"

"He will never set foot in this place again." She pushes me back against the wall. Her lips find my ear. "You could really seduce a girl with that voice." She kisses my neck. Her wet body slides against mine.

She has made me come and she has made me sing for her. I wonder what will be next.

CHAPTER TWENTY-THREE

"Where's Declan?" I ask when I come home in the evening and find just Eva on the sofa—a very unusual sight for a Friday night.

"He's out with his mates."

I quirk up my eyebrows. "You mean he's playing Dungeons and Dragons at Derek's?"

"Probably," she says with a snicker. "And I'm in need of a Caitlin James update."

She still hasn't forgiven me for bringing Caitlin here last Sunday while she wasn't home.

"Don't worry, next time she comes over, you'll be the first to know."

"So it's turning into a thing then?"

"Define thing." I sit next to her and take a sip from her wine.

"Let me get you a glass," Eva says, displaying much more courtesy than I'm used to from my housemate. "Is it getting more serious between you two?"

I have to stop myself from being snarky and asking Eva to define *serious*. "It's very early days. But, yeah, it feels great."

"So you're in a good place right now?" Eva pours me a large glass of wine.

"Yeah, I guess." I angle my body toward her so I can get a better look at her face. Something is going on here.

"I have to tell you something, Jo. I've been meaning to

for a while, but it's hard."

A lightbulb goes off in my head. "You and Declan want to move in together."

Her mouth falls open. "Yes. How did you know?"

"I'm not stupid. I was just talking to Caitlin about it the other night. Micky just asked Robin to move in with her and they haven't been seeing each other for nearly as long as you and Declan have been together. Our lease is coming up at the end of the term. Declan is here all the time. It was fully in the line of expectations."

"I just feel so bad. We've been in this flat for two years and it's been so great living together."

"Because I'm the easiest person to live with you'll ever find." I gulp down a big mouthful of wine. "Are you sure you want to live with a man? Does he put the seat down?" For all the nights Declan has spent here, he has never left any common areas less than pristine.

"Yes, I'm sure." She cocks her head. "We've seen some apartments in the area and kind of have our eye on one. It's just down the road. We'd still see each other loads."

"I'm happy that you're taking this next step in your relationship. It's a big deal." In the back of my mind, I'm already starting to figure out what to put in my "Roommate wanted" ad.

"It'll only be as of July. And I'll help you audition for a new roommate," Eva says.

"It'll be so strange to live here without you."

"I know. We'll find you someone amazing to take my place. Not as amazing as me, naturally."

"Naturally."

"Maybe you can move into Caitlin's penthouse soon," she says.

I shake my head. "Let's not get too carried away."

She twirls her wine glass between her fingers. "Have you and her, you know?"

"Slept together, you mean?" I give her a wide smile.

"Oh my God, Jo. I promise you, I'd go gay for Caitlin. For one night, oh yes." She's almost bouncing in her seat.

"You know that's a very offensive thing to say, right?"

"Not for a Gender Studies grad student," she says, chuckling. "Did she knock your socks off?"

I'm not one to tell my best friend the tiny details of my love life. Eva had no problem telling me all about her first time with Declan, but I've never told her the real reason why my previous attempts at relationships were always dead in the water before they had a chance to turn into something real.

"She's pretty amazing." That about covers it. I might not have been so enthusiastic had she asked me a few days earlier.

"As your best friend, you have to give me perks, okay?"

"You just told me you're leaving our cozy living arrangement. I don't think I have to give you anything at all."

"I'm sorry, Jo. I really am. But we can't keep living together until we're two old spinsters, so creepily close that no one will touch us."

"I'm just kidding. It's really not a big surprise."

"Are you going to be all right?" There's genuine worry on Eva's face.

"Why did you ask me if I was in a good place earlier? Did I look like I was in a bad place before?"

"You can never really tell with you. And I wasn't going to say I want to move out if things were going awry with you and Caitlin, was I?"

"I appreciate that."

"I'll make sure Declan and I have a proper dining table in our new flat so you and Caitlin can come over for intellectually-pleasing dinner parties."

"I'm sure Declan will love that."

"I made him read one of her books and he was thoroughly impressed."

"He's a good guy. I approve of him."

"He makes me happy." Eva's face goes all mushy.

I'm glad for her. It's good that she has found this sort of love. Will it ever be in the cards for me?

———

"My powers of prediction are just out of this world," I tell Caitlin the next day. "Last night, Eva told me she wants to move out so she and Declan can live together."

"Oh, I'm sorry." Caitlin has only just ushered me into her apartment. Because tomorrow is Sunday, I haven't even bothered to bring my running gear. I'd rather stay in bed with her all day.

"It's fine. I'm happy for her. It's just annoying that I'll have to find a new roommate. I really can't afford the place on my own." It feels a bit ludicrous to say this while I'm standing in Caitlin's luxurious digs.

"We'll figure something out." She takes my hands and pulls me into the living room. "Co-write that book with me and you'll get half the advance."

I chuckle. "I have a dissertation to write first."

"I get the feeling you're not taking my offer entirely seriously." She pushes me down into the sofa. "I am being deadly serious. I truly believe that if we write that book together, it would be so much better than if I wrote it alone. So much more inclusive of very important topics."

She's right. I haven't taken any of this seriously at all. How could I? She's Caitlin James and I'm only two years into getting my PhD. Maybe because we haven't had the *official meeting in my office* about it yet.

"I think you're the one who hasn't really thought this through," I say.

"We need to talk about it." She kisses my neck.

"We really do." I clasp my arms around her and pull her close, breathe her in.

"Are you staying?" she asks.

"If you'll let me." My breath has become choppy already.

"I wouldn't have it any other way." Her tongue sneaks past my lips and is lost in my mouth for long minutes. "I was so bummed I couldn't make it to your Friday afternoon class yesterday."

"Nicole was very disappointed. I'm not good enough for them anymore now that they've had a taste of you."

We lose ourselves in a kiss again. I slip my hands underneath Caitlin's blouse. Will tonight be the night? And if so, will I be able to come at her hands? Even though I have felt more confident since last Wednesday, I know full well it was only a baby step.

"I'll be there next Friday."

"Great, then I can take the afternoon off."

"If you're going to make me work for you, I will need to be paid in kind." She sinks her teeth into my earlobe.

"Ask and ye shall receive."

"How about we skip dinner and go to bed now?"

I fake a confidence I don't fully have yet. "You're asking for payment in advance?"

"I'm Caitlin James. You know I will do a good job." Her playful arrogance turns me on.

"Let's go then."

"What are you going to do to me?" Her lips are close to my ear again. Her breath on my neck.

"You'll see." I push her off me and we make our way into the bedroom. I hope she isn't expecting me to fully take charge of this. And I equally hope my *payment* isn't supposed to be an easy orgasm on my part. But I know Caitlin better now. I know what she expects of me is far less than what I expect of myself.

From the second we lie naked in bed, all I want is to delve my fingers inside of her. I want to feel her there, then use my finger on myself—if it comes to that. I want her so badly, my desire seems to be winning from my self-consciousness.

"There's no pressure in this bed," Caitlin whispers in my ear.

"I know." And I do know. Much more than the first time, when I let my fear get the upper hand so easily. "What do you want me to do?"

Caitlin is lying half on top of me, her knee pressed between my legs. Her soft skin on mine feels divine.

She pushes herself up on her elbows and stares down at me. "I want you to fuck me and look at me when you do. I don't want your face between my legs. I want it up here with me."

"That can be arranged." I smile up at her, my entire core going liquid and warm. I had no idea talking in the bedroom could have this effect—could be so easy. Perhaps it's just the effect Caitlin has on me. The effect of this journey she has taken me on.

I throw my arms around her, pull her in for a long kiss, our tongues slipping into each other's mouth, our teeth sucking at each other's lips. Even kissing feels different with her. Not that I have much experience, but either she's the world's best kisser or our lips just fit really well together.

"I might already be addicted to your breasts," she says when we break from our kiss. She's had a hand on one of them since we've landed in bed.

She takes my wrist and pushes one arm over my head, so that my right breast juts out. She then trails one fingertip all the way from my arm down to my breast, circling my nipple.

"They feel so good in my hand." There's only sincerity in her voice, as though she's worshipping my body—*my* body.

She cups her hand fully around my breast, squeezing my nipple between two fingers. I've yet to come across a hand that can gather all of my breast in it and, for once, the sight of my flesh spilling over something doesn't mortify me. It arouses me.

"Your hand feels really good there," I say, seeing as we're in a communicative mood.

Caitlin slips off me so she can bestow attention on my other breast; she repeats the process of pushing up my arm and skimming my skin with a fingertip, leaving every spot she touches with goosebumps.

When she proceeds to take a nipple between her lips and sucks it hard into her mouth, my fingers reach for the railing of her bed, holding on.

After circling my nipple with her tongue for long, delicious minutes, she looks up at me. "What do you want me to do to you?"

Oh. What *do* I want?

I'm beginning to think talking like this and giving voice to our desires might be the only way to get me where I want to be—panting at Caitlin's fingertips. And Caitlin knows. She knows so much more than I do, has lived so much more life than I have—has had so many more lovers.

When I don't immediately reply, she asks, "Can I make a suggestion?"

"I know what I want," I say.

"Okay." Her smile is wide and encouraging. "Tell me."

"Touch me while I touch myself." It comes out a bit funny, but the thing with Caitlin is that I trust her to understand and to read me in a way I can't even read myself. Because getting over myself to achieve orgasm in her bed might be a task for my mind only, but we're in this together. It's only because of her that I'm experiencing all of this, that this newfound me is even able to lie here in bed with her naked, talking about what I want. I've only known her for a few weeks and she's already got me this far. Who knows where we'll end up?

"Okay." She nods, all the while keeping a finger darting over the skin of my breasts, lightly brushing against my nipples, increasing my arousal. "Can I touch you everywhere, or just here?" She pinches a nipple between her fingers.

A moan escapes me and my lips break into an involuntary smile. "Everywhere," I say on an exhale.

She licks her lips. "You got it." Her voice is smooth as dripping honey and her whole demeanor radiates the sort of confidence that picks me up and drags me along in its slipstream, effortlessly making me believe that things I never thought were possible are.

If she hadn't just pinched my nipple, I'd have to pinch myself to believe this is real. That I'm in bed with this amazingly sexy woman, who doesn't give a damn about the patch of cellulite on her hip or the wrinkles on her face. Maybe because she's older, I feel I can let go with her more. Because if I have nothing else on her, at least I have my youth. Which isn't only lack of experience compared to her, but carries promise and things to come, wonderful, breathtaking things I don't yet know about, but that being with her can give me an inkling of.

Caitlin kisses me on the lips, while she brushes a thumb over my nipple. I feel it everywhere.

"Here I go," she whispers in my ear, a smile in her voice.

She peppers a trail of moist kisses down my cheek, my neck, my breasts, where she predictably lingers, and down to my belly-button. The action might be much the same as last time, but the effect is unmistakably different. Because I've had her eyes on me once before when I came, a lot of the pressure I put on myself the first time has been relieved. The only pressure I feel is the one building in my clit as warm blood travels toward it. It doesn't fill me with unspeakable fear this time, only with a desire I have, at last, found a voice for.

Caitlin shifts beside me and kneels between my legs. Before she can touch me again, I bring my hands down and stroke myself, my fingertips light on my wet, wet lips. She is so much closer to me than last time. I can hear her breath. I can feel the heat of her body where her legs touch mine.

I start circling my clit slowly, but I don't close my eyes. I keep them open and look at her.

"Fuck me," I whisper.

She gives a nod, shuffles closer, and skates a finger along my lips. Our hands bump into each other in a surprisingly exhilarating crash. The effect of both our hands down there, working in tandem for my pleasure, lifts me to a higher plane of arousal. I can't really see what our hands are doing, so I focus my gaze on Caitlin's face. She's looking at me, touching me, her eyes narrowed, her lips pursed. I catalog the image in my mind as the very picture of desire.

When Caitlin pushes a fingertip inside of me, I pause the motion of my own hand. I let her enter and have the sensation swoop over me. That first breach, that split second when a finger goes from outside to inside of me, has always been a huge thrill for me. Perhaps, before, because I knew it was all downhill from there. But not anymore.

To my surprise, Caitlin retracts her finger as soon as she has let it slip in.

"Let's do this a little differently," she says. She drapes her body next to mine, gluing her skin to my side, her lips close to my cheek. "I want to be here with you."

Her finger starts slipping in again, insistent from the start. I turn my head to look at her, wanting to see her face again.

"Is that good?" she asks, her voice breathy.

"Yeah." My own voice is barely audible. I bring my fingers back into the action. I touch my clit while Caitlin fucks me and it's about the most glorious sensation I've ever experienced. It feels like a double act that can only have one possible ending. Such energy geared toward only one thing: my pleasure. It's comparable to when I use my vibrator. Not so much in sensation, but in intent. When I deploy it, I know for a fact I will always come. I know it now too. There's just no other way. And I don't even need to screw my eyes shut to disappear into my mind, to conjure up images because that's what I'm used to. For the very first time, I'm so aroused that intimacy entices me more than it detracts from my pleasure.

Caitlin inches her head forward and kisses me, lets her tongue slip deep into my mouth. Her warm body is pressed hard against me, her finger is doing its work inside of me. I ratchet up the intensity of the circling motion around my clit. I buck against the movement of her hand a little, but not too much that I lose control of what my own hands are doing.

Caitlin inside of me, is what I think, on repeat, when I let go and let my climax roll over me. I stop touching myself and it's only her finger left in me, her lips lazily on mine, and my pussy contracts hard around her. The sensation intensifies my orgasm and I hear myself crying out her name.

When I come to, she's smiling broadly. Her finger is no longer inside of me and she has draped more of her body on top of me.

"Oh, damn." I break into a chuckle. "I can't believe it."

"Believe it." Her voice is soft and warm.

I want to lie here and listen to her voice forever. I want to stay in this bed with her forever. I want her to make me into a better version of me for as long as it's possible. Because that's how I feel. As though I've reached yet another new level in the game that is life. All because of her.

"Thank you." I sling an arm over her shoulder.

"I know a way for you to thank me." Her smile grows a little wicked. "I have a bit of a flooding situation going on down here."

"I'm good with those. I think I can help." I turn on my side and wrap my limbs around her.

"I can't believe how much you've given me already," she whispers when I put my head on her chest for a brief moment.

CHAPTER TWENTY-FOUR

On Monday, at the Pink Bean, I don't care about Micky's jabs. I barely hear what she has to say all morning because my mind is off to a land of its own. Caitlin James Land.

"Kristin, I think you're going to have to give Jo medical leave. She's just not functioning properly today."

As soon as she involves Kristin in the conversation, I'm snapped out of my thoughts of Caitlin. I know she's only kidding, and Kristin will surely get the joke, but I'm so used to taking my job seriously. I can't afford to lose the money it brings in—especially not now that Eva will be moving out.

"She's in love," Kristin says in that matter-of-fact tone she has. "We can cut her some slack."

This takes me aback. Am I in love?

"Did you hear that, Jo? Kristin has you all sussed out."

Maybe she has.

"May I gently remind you of how you stood behind this very counter making googly eyes at Robin from the first moment you met her."

"No way. I disliked her when she first came in here. She was so rude to me."

"She might have been rude, but I was here to witness it all. You were hot for her from the get-go."

"I truly have no idea what you are bickering about." Kristin stands in front of us at the counter. "But if it's about who's in love more, then it's ridiculous."

"Hey." Sheryl comes out of the back door. "Honey, I'm

going to need Josephine for half an hour around eleven. University business."

That's the first I've heard of that. Around eleven is when Caitlin usually comes in.

"No worries. I'll be here to step in."

"Good luck having a meeting with this woman and her absent-minded brain today. Earlier, she was stacking cups in the bottom shelf of the dishwasher. That's not where cups go," Micky says.

"Do you know what Caitlin wants to discuss with us?" Sheryl asks, ignoring Micky completely—which is the only way to deal with her sometimes.

"I have a pretty good idea, but I'll let her do all the talking."

"I hope she wants to do another guest lecture. If we can tie her down for a few, I will stand in very high regard with the Dean."

"We'll see." I quirk up my eyebrows. "Your usual?" I ask.

"Yes, please. I'll be working over there," she points at a table by the window, "until she gets here."

———

When Caitlin arrives, I all but forget about the kind of coffee I'm preparing for the next customer. Was it an Americano or a latte? I have to check the order to make sure I don't inadvertently start steaming milk.

"Hey." Even the way she greets me seems different, more gentle, more implying certain things. "Can you sit with me and Sheryl for a bit today? I would like to talk to both of you."

"Sheryl has already told me all about it." Without asking, I start preparing her flat white. "She's very curious, as am I."

"I'll take it from here." Micky takes the cup I was holding from me. "You go talk your academic talk."

Once we've sat down, Caitlin launches into her pitch.

"I want to write a book on body positivity and acceptance," she says. "After you recommended Josephine to me as an expert on the topic, I took a look at her undergrad work," Caitlin says to Sheryl, "and I would like to enlist her as co-author."

While this isn't the first I've heard of this, I feel blindsided because she is already involving Sheryl in it. She could have discussed it in more detail with me first.

"That's great," Sheryl says. "It would be great for the university as well."

'That's why I wanted to talk to you about this, Sheryl," Caitlin goes on, without waiting to hear what I have to say. I already work two jobs. I'm not sure I can swing a third one. I'm also not sure if I want to, regardless of whether I *can*. "To see if we can make her co-writing this book with me count toward her getting her PhD." She finally looks at me.

I avert my gaze and look at Sheryl instead.

"I don't see why not, though I need to run this by the proper channels, of course." Sheryl glances at me. "We'll also need to look into whether you staying on as my TA is viable if you're going to take on more work."

"Okay, look," my voice is much more firm than I had expected. "This is all well and good, but you're talking as if me co-writing this book with you is already a done deal. You haven't even asked me yet."

Caitlin cocks her head. "I thought it's what you wanted?"

"That's the problem. You thought. You jumped to a conclusion without properly asking me."

"Shall I give you two some privacy?" Sheryl is already standing up. "I'll be back in ten minutes."

"We're sitting here talking to Sheryl as if it's all a foregone conclusion. That's hardly fair," I say, trying to keep my voice low.

"You're right, Jo. I'm sorry." Caitlin pulls her chair a little closer to mine. "I wrongly assumed. Got some wires crossed in my head. Did some things in the wrong order." She puts her hands on my knees. "Will you forgive me?"

"I—I'm confused. I mean, of course I want to help you with this book, but I never asked for a co-author credit. But now you've already mentioned it to Sheryl and she's probably already mulling over ways this will make our department look good. You've not given me a choice."

"I know. I'll talk to her. I'll explain." Caitlin's palms press into my jeans.

"I'll do the talking, thank you very much. I can speak for myself perfectly."

"I'm sorry, Jo." Since when did she start shortening my name, anyway? She bats her lashes and I already feel myself warming up again, the initial coldness of my anger slipping away as if it was never there. "I stuffed up. I jumped the gun. How can I fix it?"

"By doing this properly. By telling me exactly what it is you need me to help you with. Looks like you have it all figured out already, anyway."

"I involved Sheryl because I don't want you to do this for nothing or just because the subject is important to you or because you like me. I want you to be paid for this."

"I can take care of myself."

"I never meant to imply that you couldn't. I just wanted to help."

I wave her off because that's a whole other discussion, and not one I want to jump into right now. "Are you sure it's a good idea for us to work on a book together? We've only just started seeing each other."

"Do you think it isn't?"

"I don't know. It's all going a bit fast all of a sudden."

"True, but fast can be good." She leans her body toward me. "I've taken many chances in my life. I've regretted some, but have been rewarded by most."

"You're impulsive and used to getting what you want. I'm not."

"It's just a book, Jo. Not a ring."

"A book is a big deal. To me, books mean so much more than rings." It comes out all wrong and sounds ridiculous.

"Let me explain what I have in mind, then you can decide whether you take a chance on me."

"Okay." I let her tell me about her plans for the book, and the gaps in the proposal I could fill in. The research we could do together. The outline she's working on and how she could try to convince her publisher to cooperate with the university press, stressing the win-win situation for both.

While she talks, I think of how Caitlin is entirely different than any other person I've ever met. Deep down, I'm just a simple girl from Northwood. I might have caught a glimpse of the world she travels in, but it's not my world. I'm not even thirty and she's pushing fifty. But, by god, I am in love with her. By the time she stops talking, I already know I will take a chance on her. I'd be a fool not to.

"I know I can be a bit pushy sometimes," she says. "Let me know when I'm pushing too hard."

"Do we need a safe word?" I joke, glad I can have a laugh again.

"We might do at some point." She leans in and kisses me fully on the lips.

———

"Are we in a relationship?" I ask when I see Caitlin that night. I have my reasons for doing so.

"Does it feel like a relationship to you?" We're sitting in her sofa, our legs intertwined. I'm reading a book; she's looking at her phone. I've never felt more in a relationship than right now, but I'm hardly an expert.

"It does, but I'm not sure about the conventions. How much time should have passed before you can actually call it that?"

"Does it matter?" Caitlin sure does like to reply to a question with a question. Sheryl does it too. It's what happens when you spend too much time in the Gender Studies department. "You might have noticed that I'm not one who cares much for rules and conventions."

I tip my head. "It's hard to miss." I hook my hands behind her knees and pull her closer to me. "Which is another thing I wanted to talk about."

"Let me guess?" Caitlin shuffles around to find her balance. She draws her knees into her chest, but puts her hand on mine. "Now that you feel we're in a relationship, you want to set some boundaries."

"It would be good to be on the same page."

"Agreed." She looks at our hands, then cuts her eyes back at me. "From experience, I can tell you that when I'm in the falling-in-love stage of a relationship, no other women interest me. It's only normal that all my attention is focused on you." She gives my fingers a little squeeze. "And I am. Right now. In that very stage."

My tummy does a funny tumble. Good god. Caitlin James is falling in love with me.

"Me too," I mumble. "Very much so."

"Excellent start to our *relationship*."

"Couldn't be better." I pick up her hand and kiss a knuckle.

"I also know from experience that it's not realistic to expect this feeling to last forever, even though most everyone is so desperate to hang onto it."

"Is that when your relationships usually open up?"

"Sometimes. Sometimes not. It really all depends." She smiles sheepishly. "I might come across as one, but I'm not the biggest expert on all the formalities. To me, it's an organic process. Respect for the other and, as you said earlier, being on the same page, is of paramount importance."

"Have you ever fallen in love with someone who wasn't much into having an open relationship?"

"Quite a few times."

"And?" I prod.

"It didn't work out." Caitlin looks at me from under her lashes. "Which was sometimes very painful."

"So your freedom is more important to you than your feelings for your partner?"

"No." Caitlin shakes her head, possibly to give her reply more strength. "It's not about my freedom. It's about who I am. I have never believed that two people can satisfy each other on every level for the rest of their lives. I've never bought into the sanctity of marriage and I'll-love-you-and-only-you forever bullshit. It's a made-up restriction that has ruined many a life."

"But from what you tell me, your convictions have ruined many promising relationships?"

"I don't see it that way. How can a relationship be promising or good or respectful of both partners if they don't see eye to eye on such a fundamental principle?" She strokes my palms with her thumb. "I used to be very militant about this stuff." She chuckles. "Just ask Sheryl. I drove her crazy with my rants against monogamy. I've calmed down a lot since then."

"But how does it work practically?" I press on. "When you both live in the same city? Some nights you just don't come home?"

"That has happened, but very rarely." She slants her head. "Sometimes we had threesomes. Or we went to a play party. Things like that. It's not about the thrill of doing something behind your partner's back, which is really what most philanderers are after. Take away that bit, and it all becomes a whole lot less enticing. For me, non-monogamy is about keeping an important part of yourself alive: sexual desire. But it's still something most people are not willing to address because they believe they can find everything they need with their partner, and some do, or think they do, and that's great, but that's not me. I don't believe in fairy-tales like that."

I ponder this, nodding, lost in thought. Play parties? Threesomes? Is all of this in my future?

"I know it's a lot to think about, but all of this is such a gradual process. All you really need, right now, is an open mind, Josephine. I'm not asking you to commit to anything that might not be your thing."

"I kind of disagree." The mere thought of Caitlin with another woman while we're together feels like a punch in the stomach. "I'm falling in love with you. I want to be with you. And even though I can't predict whether this will work or not, my intention is for this to last. That's what I will put my energy into. So it's only fair for me to know what will happen in a few months or years or I don't know how long, when you propose we open up the relationship."

Caitlin nods. "I get where you're coming from. I totally do. But it can't be my task to pressure you into something you don't want or can't believe in. Doing something that goes against your own value system should not be a price to pay for being with me and what I believe in. But, and this might be the most important thing of all, that's why we communicate. We talk about our feelings every step of the way."

"Before I met you, I had never even considered it. I did briefly when I read some books on the subject for my course work, but I never even once thought any of that would ever apply to me."

"Why was that your initial thought?"

"Because… I don't know. It's just not how I thought or dreamed about a relationship. Truth be told, I've never had to think about romantic relationships much in my life. I'm almost thirty and I've had two that I can call that and they lasted less than a year. Right now, to me, it kind of feels like we're on two different levels here. I'm only a beginner and you seem so advanced."

"That only means we can learn a lot from each other. Not just you from me, but I can learn from you as well. I have already learned from being with you."

"Really? What have you learned from me?" She must be joking.

"You taught me a valuable lesson this morning, when you told me off for acting too fast without consulting you."

"But that's a general thing. That was just correcting a mistake, something we do every day, no matter who we are with."

"Yes, but I was in that circumstance because I was with you. Someone else might not have spoken up, or would have just gone with the flow because I was talking about co-writing and book deals. Your convictions shone through for me in that moment. I think that's a beautiful thing."

"Hm." I don't really know what to say to that. I feel like I'm only skirting the edges of truly understanding what she's trying to say. I'm attracted to it but I'll have to go up a few more levels before I can see it all for myself. I need more experiences. More life behind me. More talks like this.

"Think about this." Caitlin has scooted closer. "When two people who love each other, respect each other and have wide open lines of communication about their feelings, what can really go wrong?" She pulls her lips into a smile and narrows her eyes. I can tell she wants to kiss me.

"If you put it in utopian words like that." Her nearness is putting a spell on me again.

"It doesn't have to be impossible. For me, it's the basis of any relationship. It's why I never see my family. Because they don't respect me. For me, nothing is more important in life than respect and I base every important decision on it."

"I respect you," I say, leaning in.

"I respect you too." Our lips meet in a kiss and it hits me that one of the reasons I was so attracted to Caitlin from the very beginning, apart from being a fan girl, is because she was so respectful toward me—which is not a given for a girl like me.

CHAPTER TWENTY-FIVE

"Do you know the very first thing the great Caitlin James said to me when we met?" Kristin is looking at me with glee in her eyes.

"Should I guess?" I ask.

"Oh, here we go." Caitlin mock-sighs.

"She asked, in all seriousness, whether I shaved my legs." Kristin chuckles. "I was so nervous about meeting Sheryl's friends for the first time and up comes this chick and, out of the blue, asks me this question. Of course, the shit really hit the fan when I said that, yes, I do as a matter of fact shave my legs."

"Caitlin shaves her legs now," I say to Kristin. "They're so smooth, you wouldn't believe it." I don't even try to suppress my laughter. Kristin and Sheryl are a goldmine of information on Caitlin.

"That was twenty years ago. And I still believe most women shave their legs for all the wrong reasons," Caitlin says.

"Why do you shave yours now, then?" Sheryl asks.

"I'm courting," Caitlin says matter-of-factly.

I burst out in a giggle.

"That's the reason?" Sheryl continues to grill her. "So before you came back to Sydney and met Jo, you weren't shaving them?"

"Okay, fine. I was. I'm just as shallow as everyone else. I shave my legs because I like how it feels when I moisturize and—"

"You moisturize as well?" Kristin jabs Sheryl in the arm. "Did you hear that, babe? Caitlin is not as immune to the marketing powers of the cosmetics industry as we always believed she was."

"Winters on the east coast of America leave you no choice," Caitlin says, a laconic smile on her face.

"She has gone soft. Caitlin James has lost her fire and is no longer on the barricades. It must be what a modicum of fame stateside does to you," Sheryl says.

"You're right. I have crumbled under the pressures of our misogynistic, consumerist society. I should do penance by starting a retreat for women where they can escape the demands of modern life and live without being constantly pinged by their phones, or asked to dress up nicely so they can make their man look good. I'm on it," Caitlin says in her lecturing tone.

"Can you believe that was almost twenty years ago?" Sheryl asks, going soft herself.

"Twenty years ago, I was only eight years old," I say.

All three of them shake their head at me. "What are you doing here having dinner with us on a Friday night, Josephine?" Sheryl jokes. "You should be out clubbing."

"The parties we threw when we were your age," Caitlin chimes in.

"All for the cause," Kristin says.

"There aren't many things I find more ludicrous than standing in a dark room with a bunch of strangers listening to music that's too loud. It's just not my thing," I say.

"Josephine prefers staying home to read Caitlin James books." Caitlin puts her arm around my shoulders. "That will always be our origin story." She's not shy about public displays of affection—though we are in the privacy of Kristin and Sheryl's apartment—and pecks me on the cheek.

"Next year you'll be holding a book with your own name on it," Sheryl says, pride in her voice.

"Maybe," I say. "We'll see."

"I'll set up a meeting with my publisher soon," Caitlin says.

"I won't be able to keep you as a barista if you keep moving up in the world like that," Kristin says.

"Trust me, you will. You're the best boss anyone can hope for."

"Hey," Sheryl says.

"You are, too, of course. You're both equals in every way."

"Are you sure Kristin isn't nicer than Sheryl?" Caitlin asks, a big grin on her face.

"No. They're both equally great." These two women have changed so much for me. Sheryl by being the sort of professor and mentor I was so drawn to intellectually, I knew from the bat I wanted her as my masters' thesis supervisor. Kristin for giving me a well-paid job in the Pink Bean, even though I had no experience.

"If it wasn't for me, you would never have met Caitlin," Sheryl says.

"I guess I have to give her that one." I put up my hands and smile apologetically at Kristin.

"That's all right. I'm not interested in being better at anything than Sheryl."

"You're always so zen, babe," Sheryl says.

"Of course—I'm Korean." Kristin says it in such a dead-pan way we all burst out laughing.

"And I love you." It's Sheryl's turn to give Kristin a quick kiss. When I look at them I can't help but wonder about their relationship. I know they've had their ups and downs, but they seem so settled now. So content with just each other. And as far as I know, they don't have an open relationship. I wish I could pull back the curtain and catch a glimpse of their true private life. I wish I had more experience at relationships before going further in this one with Caitlin. As much as I love being with her, and as much as she has had a positive effect on me already, I'm still carrying around a good amount of fear.

Twenty years from now, will it be Caitlin and me entertaining friends in our home like this? A lifetime of love between us, and all of it so easily visible on our faces?

———

On Saturday afternoon, I decide to finally take Amber up on her offer of a free private yoga lesson. With Caitlin in the picture, I've been missing quite a few morning runs, so I see it as a peace offering to my body. Caitlin has done a few of her classes and she keeps raving about them. She tried to teach me a few yoga poses herself but it's just too distracting when she does it. We always end up doing anything but yoga —though nothing that has allowed me to come without having my own hands at work between my legs.

Maybe yoga will help with that, too.

Amber ushers me into a small room of which one of the walls is all mirrors, making me feel uncomfortable from the get-go. I'm wearing faded running pants that contrast heavily with her trendy yoga kit—funky-striped pants and a tank top so tight I can see her abs through the fabric.

"I'm so glad you came," she says, and puts a gentle hand on my shoulder.

"I can't say the same just yet," I joke. "But thanks for doing this, no matter how I feel about it later."

"Don't be nervous. It's just you and me. More often than not, what keeps people from the yoga mat is the perceived judgement of the others in the class. There's none of that here."

Amber rolls out two mats, then turns to me. "Things seem to be going well between you and Caitlin," she says, kind of out of the blue.

"Yeah. Pretty well."

"That's really great." I sense some hesitation in her tone.

"I get the distinct impression a *but* is supposed to

follow that statement."

"I just don't want you to get hurt, that's all."

"I appreciate that." I would very much like to avoid that also. "Did she, er, actually hurt you back then?"

"Maybe not so much hurt me as threw me off balance for a while."

I make a mental note to quiz Caitlin about how she treated Amber and how that aligns with her policy of respect above anything. From Amber's point of view, which is the only one I have, Caitlin's behavior toward her wasn't very respectful at all.

"You don't have to worry about me, Amber. I can handle myself."

"I know you can. You'll be able to handle yourself even better after this session with me." She draws her face into a solemn expression. "Shall we start?"

"Does it begin with *Ohm*?" I ask, grinning.

"No. I'll keep the more spiritual things for later."

We sit down in lotus position and for the next hour Amber teaches me the basics of yoga and, in the process, has me bend my body in ways I never deemed possible.

At the end of the lesson, when she has me in something called *shavasana*, which is basically just lying down with my eyes closed, I conclude that, though challenging for my inflexible body, this yoga class was an enjoyable way to spend an hour. But I'm more the kind of person to practice it alone in my room, now that she has given me some of the basics, rather than ever set foot in a studio filled with people like Amber, or Caitlin, or Micky. And I look forward to my next run, though I'm unsure I'll be able to move at all tomorrow.

———

Later that day, Caitlin and I are sitting on her balcony, a bottle of wine between us.

"There's an open mic again next Friday," she says.

"Do you want to go?" It could be fun to go with her

again, look at her as she reads another poem, and notice all the differences between now and the first time she did it. It could be a good progression barometer of our relationship. "Read another poem?"

"I would like to go, yes, but not to read a poem." She pours some more wine into my glass. "This morning, when you were in the shower, I overheard you sing, and I swear to you, Josephine, it touched me on some deep emotional level. I had tears in my eyes."

I try to remember what I was singing this morning. The song escapes me. Perhaps because I'm more focused on the image of Caitlin standing outside the bathroom door, listening to me.

"Honestly, Jo. You have a gift. There's such strength in your voice. You could move so many people with it."

"I'm not really interested in moving many people." Only Caitlin will do just fine.

"I'm serious. A voice like that. You can't just keep that to yourself."

"I believe I very much can."

"Well, yes, I know you can, but why would you want to? I was standing outside and the water was running and even then, I could so clearly hear what you were putting into it and how you meant the words you were singing. It was so beautiful."

"I'm very flattered, but I have two things to say about this and then I would like to talk about something else. One: you *would* find it beautiful because, you know, er, you and I…" How can I refer to us without sounding too forward? "We're together. We're in love. That makes everything sound better. Second, I'm not someone who likes to take to the stage. It's not me. I don't enjoy it."

"You enjoy teaching."

"That's not the same thing at all."

"Then let me ask you this: what are you so afraid of?"

"I think this might be one of the instances where

you're pushing too hard."

"Oh." She leans back in her chair, retreating. "Understood. But will you please just think about it? Just consider it. I think it might be good—"

I hold up a hand. "Please."

"Okay, we'll change the subject. Meanwhile, I'll have you and your voice all to myself." She sends me a smile but I can tell it's not her widest, most convincing one.

"My turn to ask you a question," I say.

"Shoot. I'll answer anything without inhibitions." Her smile grows a bit more confident.

"Amber still seems kind of hung up on that time you slept together." It feels so strange to say this. "Do you think you treated her respectfully enough?"

Caitlin ponders this for a moment, but doesn't seem too taken aback by my question. "If she's still talking about it now, then I probably didn't." She gazes into the night sky. "Being respectful is definitely the mantra I try to live by the most, but just like any other human being, I sometimes screw up. That's the nature of life. I've yet to meet a single person who doesn't have regrets."

"Do you regret sleeping with her?"

"No, but I regret not being clear on my intentions." She holds up her wine glass. "Most of my regrets can probably be tracked down to too much of this."

"Ah, too much booze: the catch-all for our worst mistakes." Another question pops into my head, but to be able to properly push the words from my mouth, I need another sip of wine first. "I have another question." My voice sounds more coy than I would like it to.

"Yes?" Caitlin has a grin on her face. She likes this. She likes opening herself up to me, no holds barred.

"How many women have you slept with?" I don't know why, but I avert my gaze as soon as the words have left my lips. As though I don't really want to know the answer.

I hear her shuffling in her chair. "Does a number really

matter that much to you?"

I turn to look at her again. "I don't know. I'm just curious."

"Understandable, I guess." She sits up a little straighter. "If you really want to know the number, I could tell you, but I'd have to look in my diary first. I'm not really in the habit of keeping count."

"Your diary?"

She nods solemnly. "Yes, I write in it every single day and have done so for more than twenty years. Cheapest therapy I've ever had."

"Every time you slept with someone, you made a note of it?"

"Sleeping with someone is quite a significant action, don't you think? One that merits a mention in my journal."

I'm suddenly very curious to know if and what she has written about me.

"Do you, er… rate us. I mean, them?" I stammer.

"What?" She shakes her head. "Where on earth would you get that idea?"

"I don't know. It just… came out."

"I truly do wonder what goes on in that head of yours." Her face has softened. "But just for the record, you have not been rated. It's a journal. Not some system to measure sexual prowess. It's just a way to clear my head and to work through things I have on my mind. I hardly ever reread what I have written, unless I'm in a very self-indulgent mood." She snickers. "I highly recommend the practice. It's great for unburdening yourself."

"Between you and Amber, I feel like I've been in touch with two gurus today."

"She's a good teacher." Caitlin remains serious. "Do you think I should apologize to her? She hasn't said anything to me about it since I've returned. I truly believed we were okay."

"That's up to you." My mind is no longer on Amber

and whether Caitlin treated her respectfully enough. I can't stop thinking about Caitlin's diary and what I wouldn't give to sneak a peek into the entry of the day she met me.

CHAPTER TWENTY-SIX

The next afternoon, I'm still at Caitlin's. I've barely been able to move all day, which appears to be a great source of delight for her.

"If this is what yoga does to your body, I'll gladly stick to running," I say.

"It's only the first time. Next time, you'll feel good as new the morning after." Caitlin stands behind me while I'm sitting in the sofa, her hands on my shoulders. "Would the young lady like a little shoulder massage?"

"That would be amazing."

She sinks her thumbs into a particularly painful knot in my shoulder. "You're so tense."

"I'm in pain. I need a new body."

"I know exactly what you need." She gives my shoulder the lightest of squeezes then, disappointingly, retracts her hands. "I'm going to run you a nice hot bath and then I'll give you a proper massage." She puts a funny inflection into the word *proper*. "It's Sunday. The day of relaxation."

My muscles are so sore, I barely make it into the bath she has drawn for me. But when I sink into the hot embrace of the water, a fraction of tension seems to leave my muscles immediately.

"I'm never coming out of this bath again. It's too divine," I say to Caitlin who balances on the lip of the tub.

"I'm sure you'll change your mind when the water gets cold. But do take your time. I'll be patiently waiting." She runs a finger through the water, until it reaches my breast, and lets it skim along my wet skin, then stops at my nipple. She leaves her finger there while she bends over and kisses me softly on the lips. A few seconds later, she has left the bathroom and it's just me, my painful muscles, and a surge of desire spiking in my belly.

While I soak for as long as I feel comfortable keeping her waiting for me, I think about how quickly all of this has become easy. How I don't think about covering my body anymore when we're together. How I let her strip me of my clothes and help me into the bath. How arousal has pushed self-consciousness away as though there's no room for the two to co-exist within me anymore.

By the time I drag myself out of the bath, the water is still pleasantly warm. Caitlin's promised massage is much more alluring than being immersed in water, no matter how relaxed it makes my tortured muscles feel.

"That was fast." Caitlin is waiting for me in the bedroom fully undressed.

"What kind of massage do you plan on giving me?" A smile appears on my face.

"Full body, of course."

Even though my skin hasn't fully dried up yet, I drop the towel and rush to her side.

"Lie on your belly," she says.

I happily agree. I stretch out and put my hands underneath the pillow. Everything is soft around me and I eagerly await Caitlin's first touch.

I hear her shuffle around on the sheets, then feel her hip press into my side. A finger skates along my spine and my skin already breaks out into goosebumps. Another finger follows the previous one's path until I feel both of her hands on my shoulders. She digs her thumbs into my flesh again and I let out a little groan. There is no sign of any massage oil, which confirms my suspicion that Caitlin's prime objective is not to give me a massage at all.

Her fingers ripple over the line of my shoulders, relieving some tension momentarily, only to have it replaced by sexual anticipation. I can hardly believe how easily I let it grab hold of me now. If I had followed my instinct, and Caitlin hadn't been so gracious and patient with me, I wouldn't be in this bed right now, with her hands all over me. I would be at home, miserable, thinking of what could have been.

I feel her lips on the nape of my neck. The soft, wet kiss she plants there feels like she just kissed a nipple. The contact travels through me and leaves my belly tingling and my entire body aching for so much more.

Over the past few weeks, we've become quite adept at both our hands working in tandem toward my climax. In a way, it's frustrating how simple it has become, because it makes me think of all the missed opportunities I've had. Then again, perhaps it was my psyche's way of waiting until someone like Caitlin came along. Someone who swept me off my feet so swiftly that my anxiety didn't have much chance to intervene.

Caitlin's kisses descend down my spine. Her hair tickles my back. This is better than any massage. In fact, I think all muscle soreness has miraculously disappeared. Caitlin's hands and lips truly are magical. She kisses me all over my back, then changes position. She nudges my legs apart and not being able to see what she's up to only increases my arousal. My clit is thumping wildly and I feel the familiar tingle of extreme arousal between my legs.

Caitlin drapes her body over mine until her mouth is near my ear. "Your full body massage, Madam," she whispers. She kisses my neck again and an arrow of lust shoots up from my pussy to every last cell of my body. Then I feel her nipples skim along my back. Slowly, she traces some pattern that's impossible to recognize and I melt into the mattress a little more.

Her nipples graze my ass cheeks and soon after I feel

her lips there, kissing every last patch of skin. She ends with one final peck, then shifts positions again and comes to lie next to me. I turn on my side to look at her.

"How was that for a massage?" she asks, a proud smile on her face.

"Not that relaxing," I say. "You've got me in quite a state."

"Yeah?" She scoots closer, her hand reaching for my breast. "What state is that?"

"Very hot and bothered."

"That was the idea." She leans in and kisses me. Her kiss is insistent from the get-go, the dance of her tongue in my mouth doesn't leave any room for misinterpretation. It's one of the things I've come to love about her the most. Her utter lack of hesitation. Her uncompromising views on desire—no matter how they might affect our relationship in the future. The ways in which she makes me feel so wanted —a foreign concept to me until not so long ago.

Her other hand is on the back of my neck, pulling me close. My hands skim along the small gap between our bodies, until one comes to rest on her breast. It's a thrill to be brushing a thumb over her nipple while she does the exact same thing to me—an enthralling mirror sensation. It gives me an idea.

I'll have to try some time and I'm already so aroused. All the memories of when I fucked her rush back to me, and the accompanying flutters of passion they ignited in me. Right now, in my life, there is nothing more enticing than slipping a finger inside of Caitlin. Fucking her and watching her while I do so, the way she asked me to. It's the pinnacle of intimacy, to be able to let go like that, under your lover's gaze. I want to try. I want to see what it does to me when we both do it.

"Fuck me while I fuck you," I say on an exhale.

She arches up her eyebrows. "Okay," she whispers.

We kiss again and this time her hand is firmer on my

breast, more intentional and hungrier. This is the very thing that has helped me to relax around her so much. Her obvious hunger for me. It forced me to rethink some long-held beliefs about myself and the undesirability of my body. This is what Caitlin has done for me. Her actions have shown me what no words could ever tell me—words my rational mind could never accept without hard evidence.

All the evidence I need is in this bed right now. It's in the way her breath comes in short, shallow bursts when we break for air. In the way her eyes narrow with desire when she looks at me. The fire in them, the blatant yearning.

"Spread your legs," she says, as she spreads hers.

My hand dives down instantly at the sight of her there, at the prospect of pushing inside of her. Her hand does the same. If her desire for me is only a fraction of the lust I feel for her in this moment, it's already more than plenty. Enough for me. Because my lust is boundless, ever-renewable, unquenchable.

She runs a finger over my sex. It glides over the soft flesh of my lips.

"I love this," she says. "There's so much promise in this action."

I can only agree. My own finger is busy exploring her lips. On the same path it has been down so many times before.

She doesn't dilly-dally, but pushes high inside of me.

"Oh," I moan, looking into her eyes. I need to take a second before I can follow suit, but it doesn't take me long to recover. She's waiting for me. We're going to do this together.

As always, I relish the moment my finger slips between her wet folds. It always feels like such a privilege. But more than that, it's the most effective action to get my clit throbbing out of control.

She starts thrusting first. I try to match her rhythm, try to find an alternate motion that suits us both. It's easy when we look into each other's eyes like that. At least, it seems so. Effortless and maddeningly effective at the same time.

"This is so hot," she whispers.

I can only utter a groan in reply. In the weeks we've been together, Caitlin's taken me on a journey along ever-increasing levels of arousal. Here we are. A notch higher once again.

This isn't a matter of letting go, anymore. It's a matter of hanging on. As though all the orgasms I missed by being too inside my head, too uptight, too insecure and hateful of my body, are catching up with me. As if they've banded together to teach me a lesson and say, "See. What was so hard about that?"

As much as I might be ultimately responsible for my own climax, this is one we're creating together, in perfect unison. Her fingers inside of me and mine inside her. Every time she thrusts up, her thumb brushes against my clit, until she stops her thrusting motion and changes it into a more minute but intense movement inside of me, allowing her thumb better access to my aching clit.

"Oh Christ," I mutter. For a moment, I'm so undone by her eyes on me, her fingers everywhere, that I forget my own fingers' duties. The instant I remember that I'm still inside of her, it pushes me over an invisible edge—the very thing that only ever exists in the mind and has kept me from so much joy. It's ridiculously easy to ride into my climax on her finger while her thumb fondles my clit. Her warmth envelops me, inside and out. A smile spreads on my face and she mirrors it. I have no idea if she's even close to coming. Maybe it's not even humanly possible. All I know is that I am. I'm coming at Caitlin's fingers. She's got me. I'm all hers now. It has finally happened.

"Keep fucking me," she whispers as her fingers retreat. "Don't stop."

I give her all I have, hoping it's enough after what just occurred. As it turns out, Caitlin making me come like that only spurs me on. I fuck her until she comes, mere minutes after I did.

CHAPTER TWENTY-SEVEN

By Friday, I've been singing the same song in the shower every morning. I hum it in the corridors at the university and, ditching the podcasts, listen to it on repeat when I go for my morning run. I haven't committed to anything, but by the time the open mic starts and Kristin starts taking names for performances, I know that, if I were to feel like it, I would be ready, because I know the song by heart. Not just the words, but the melody is part of me. The notes live within me. The inflections of its vowels have a permanent place in my brain. If I ever do sing a song in front of an audience, this will be the one.

I don't give my name to Kristin. I want to see how the evening plays out. Robin's colleague Meredith is here but Micky and Robin aren't. Sheryl is present, of course, but most of the other people are nothing more than acquaintances, which might help when the time comes to make my final decision.

Caitlin hasn't talked anymore about me singing tonight. I don't know if she suspects that I might go for it, but if she does, she hasn't let on. She hasn't given her name to Kristin either.

As I sit through the first two performances, I think about all the things that have changed. I feel like a different person than the last time I sat at this table with Caitlin and Sheryl for an open mic night. For someone who had convinced herself that having an orgasm was optional, being able to achieve one has led to a surprising boost in my confidence. Sometimes, when I'm running and I spot someone looking at me funnily, I think to myself, "And are you sleeping with Caitlin James? Is she making you come on a regular basis?" It's silly, but it works. I care much less about pitying glances and when I've missed a morning run because Caitlin's presence kept me in bed, I can now go for a jog on a Saturday afternoon, when the streets are much more crowded, and the looks of others could annoy me so much more. But they don't. Because when I get a look now, I don't just feel like fat Josephine anymore.

Next week, I will sign a contract with Caitlin's publisher to co-write a book with her. And in the evenings, when I crawl into bed with her, it's no longer terror that grips my heart in its fist, but delicious, warm love. And sometimes, when I look in the mirror, I can even catch a glimpse of the woman Caitlin says she finds so beautiful. I can look into my own eyes and not dismiss them as not pretty enough to make up for the unappealing body I live in.

"The next brave soul to confront the open mic is Ramona," Kristin announces. "She is going to sing 'Hey Jude' for us."

Ramona is a tiny woman—I'm easily triple her size—with a beautifully fragile voice.

"She's good, but you could do so much better," Caitlin whispers in my ear mid-song, and keeps her mouth close to me for an instant.

"It's not a competition," I reply. And while this evening is definitely not about who's better than who, a part of me does kind of feel like besting her.

"Of course it's not, babe," Caitlin says, and leans back in her chair.

When I look at her she has a smug smile on her face. Maybe she does know. Or perhaps she has picked up on the changes in me. Maybe I'm more transparent than I think I am.

After Ramona, a woman in dreads with the most intense blue eyes reads an angry short story about a mother and a daughter who don't understand each other. It's strangely moving, perhaps because of the way she performs it instead of just reading it, and then it's Kristin's turn again, who asks, "Any more takers for the mic tonight?"

There's a brief silence. My heart pounds in my chest. I lock eyes with Kristin and raise my hand.

"Our very own Josephine," she says.

"I'm so proud of you," Caitlin whispers as, on trembling legs, I stand up.

I walk to the front and take the mic from Kristin. I'd rather she not say too much anymore.

"Did you bring a backing track?" Kristin asks.

"I'll be fine like this."

She nods and hurries to her seat on the side. I wait until she has sat down. Should I say something? So many eyes on me. The very picture of what used to be my worst nightmare. Have I truly changed so much that I can do this? Will the notes not die a slow, excruciating death in the back of my throat as soon as I open my mouth to sing?

"Hi, I'm Josephine Greenwood," I say sheepishly. "I'm going to sing you a song."

I look at Caitlin, who seems to be sitting on the edge of her seat. She gives me a thumbs-up and it's all I need. Not because I'm standing up here for her. I'm here for me.

I clear my throat, try to loosen my shoulders as best I can, and launch into the first line of a slowed-down version of "Bird on the Wire".

The first chorus I sing with my eyes closed, but after that I slowly open them, letting the audience in. Letting them truly see me. Caitlin has her hands clasped in front of her mouth. She's the only person I see in the small crowd. All my focus is on her, hoping the song will convey how sorry I am for all the mistakes I made in the beginning and all the ones I've yet to make.

By the time I hit the last, low note, a tear streams down my cheek.

"Thank you," I say.

Every single person rises from their seat and applauds me for long minutes. It's heart-warming for the first few seconds, but quickly becomes embarrassing.

"Thank you so much," I mumble into the microphone and put it on the nearest table.

Caitlin has made her way to me and throws her arms around me, as though I just scored the winning goal in a very tense football match.

"I don't even know what to say." She holds my hand tightly in hers.

"You've done it." Sheryl has sidled up to us. "You've managed to shut Caitlin up."

Kristin joins us. "Eva wasn't lying when she said you could sing. Blimey." She puts a hand between my shoulder blades and leaves it there for a lingering second.

"Spectacular," Sheryl says. "Forget about writing a book with Caitlin. You're a star, Jo."

Caitlin remains quiet. She just stands there, holding my hand, looking at me as if I just landed from another planet.

"Come here for a minute." She ignores the others and drags me into a corner of the Pink Bean. She takes my other hand in hers as well and stares at me. "I love you for doing that. For being brave and facing your fears head-on." She looks straight into my eyes. "I love you."

I swallow a sudden lump out of my throat. "I love you too." This is no moment for sarcastic comments. This is Caitlin telling me she loves me. And all the time I was singing, I couldn't think of anything else but how much I love her.

CHAPTER TWENTY-EIGHT

"I have an early birthday present for you," Caitlin says, out of the blue. It's just a regular Wednesday morning in the Pink Bean and my birthday is not for a couple of months. Getting presents was the furthest thing from my mind, though I have been agonizing over what to get Caitlin for her birthday, which is coming up soon. I can't spend a lot of money—and Caitlin has every last thing her heart desires already anyway. I was secretly hoping we would strike a fashionable non-consumerist agreement of bowing out of getting each other presents, but seeing as she got me an early one, I guess I'll have to step up to the plate.

"Really?" I wasn't raised to have many materialistic aspirations and it's true what they say: it's the thought that counts more than anything. In this case, I can hardly believe that Caitlin has spent time thinking about getting *me* a present.

"I have a little speech to deliver before I can give it to you. If I may?" She bows her head solemnly.

"I wouldn't expect anything else."

"I usually think mutual gift-giving is just another ridiculous way of inflicting even more stress on an already stressed-out society at occasions like birthdays and Christmas. Who truly needs more stuff? What I do believe in, however, is surprising your loved ones with small tokens of affection—and this bit is really important—without expecting anything in return."

"I tend to agree with your vision." The only person I consistently send presents is my sister, and that's more out of guilt because I can't be there with her for most special occasions.

"Keeping all of that in mind." She delves into her purse and takes out what looks like an envelope but is made out of gift wrap paper. "For you."

I raise my eyebrows while I tear at the wrapper. No matter anyone's stance on the sanity of gift-giving, it is thrilling to receive one.

I slip out what can really only be a voucher for something. I blink and look at a plane ticket with my name printed on it.

"It's a flexible ticket. You can change the dates if you want to. But I thought you might want to go home next weekend."

Caitlin is sending me home for my sister's birthday.

"Oh my god." When I look up at her, I have tears in my eyes. "Bea will be over the moon."

"I know how much she means to you."

I put the ticket on the table and rise so I can wrap my arms around her.

"Thank you so much," I whisper, my lips wet against her neck.

"You're very welcome." Caitlin holds me tightly.

When we break from our hug and sit back down again, I can't stop a persistent smile from spreading on my face.

"I meant what I said, Jo. You don't have to give me anything for my birthday. You've given me so much already."

I chuckle. I could argue with her. Give her a list of everything she has given me that wasn't bought with money. But I'm so elated to be going home that I just nod.

"Besides, you've given me the best gift already. Not only hearing, but seeing you sing as well. That was priceless. You should really do that again some time."

After my performance at the open mic, Caitlin told me

so many times I looked breathtaking while I was singing, I'm almost ready to start believing her.

"I can't wait to tell Bea tomorrow morning." The prospect of my sister's laugh—so genuine and pure—in my ear pushes another shot of adrenalin into my veins. "Although this does mean we will be spending a weekend apart." I purse my lips together.

"Or... I could book another ticket. One with my name on it."

"Really? You want to go spend time in the sticks?"

"I want to see where you grew up and meet your family. Unless you plan on keeping me a secret, of course." A grin spreads on her face.

I could really be with all the people I love at the same time? The mere thought of it causes a prickle of tears behind my eyes.

"I could never keep you a secret." I stand up again, wrap my arms around her anew. "You're too amazing for that."

———

After my shift, Kristin has asked me to join her upstairs. I still have to ask her to take a day off next week, but I figure I'd better hear what she has to say first.

"The open mic nights have been so successful, I've been thinking about doing something at the Pink Bean every Friday," Kristin says as soon as we've sat down. "It's good for business."

"That's a great idea." Instantly, my mind goes in the direction of an extra Friday evening shift. It could work. It's after office hours. Of course, these days, I'm dating. I usually spend Friday nights with Caitlin. But between an extra shift every week and the complicated structure Caitlin and I are trying to come up with for an advance on royalties, it may mean I won't need to look for another roommate.

"I've been brainstorming possible concepts. The open mic is good for once a month, but I wouldn't want to do more of them. I think variety might be the key. I was thinking about a comedy night. Definitely something LGBT-related. Maybe ask Caitlin to host a debate some time."

"I'm sure she'd be up for that. Some people don't need that much coaxing to be in the spotlight." I shoot her a smile. I'm still filled with good cheer after my weekend plans have so abruptly changed. "If you want to add some extra star power, you could invite Zoya to take part as well."

Kristin nods. "Imagine the three of them taking questions from the audience: Sheryl, Caitlin, and Zoya."

"Full house guaranteed." I find her eyes. "I can work the extra shift. Perhaps not every single Friday evening, but most. Maybe we can work out a schedule with Alyssa."

"Oh no, Josephine. That's not what I wanted to ask you."

"Oh." Serves me right for being too presumptuous. "I just figured."

"I want to ask you something else."

"Okay?" My palms are beginning to sweat. Is this an impromptu performance review? If so, it would be a first.

"I would love to have an evening with Josephine Greenwood once in a while. Just you and your voice. Well, we'd need someone on guitar or keyboard or whatever you might need. But I think it could become a real draw."

"Me?" I shake my head. "No way."

"Jo, I was in the audience when you sang one song. I saw the effect you had on every single person in the room. It was pure emotion."

"You want me to sing." I have to repeat it to believe it. "But what would I even sing?"

"Sing anything you want. Sing the songs that move you the most, that bring you the most joy. Quite frankly, you could sing children's songs and people would still love it."

"It took a lot for me to get up there and sing that one song. I don't think I could do what you're asking of me."

"It's just an idea for the future. We can work on this

together. You don't have to perform a full show. Just sing a few songs and make people feel good. That's what I want customers to associate with the Pink Bean. That tingly feeling of everything being right, if just for a brief moment of their day. The way you sing evokes that so effortlessly."

"I—I'm very flattered, but I need to think about it."

"Of course. And you will be paid for this, of course. I'm not asking you to consider doing this for free. Just to be clear."

"Wow. What a day." I lean back in my chair. "Full of surprises." I already want to call Caitlin. She'll try to convince me to say yes. Maybe I need to decide for myself first.

"Isn't life amazing sometimes?" Kristin sits there beaming a smile at me in her very Kristin way. Legs held together ladylike. Not a hair out of place. When I first started working in the Pink Bean, I would never have dreamed we'd become friends, let alone that she'd make me a proposition like this.

"Oh, yes." I nod and, maybe for the first time in my life, fully agree.

CHAPTER TWENTY-NINE

During the past month, one of Kristin's phrases has sat in the back of my brain at all times. What she said about when I sang at the Pink Bean open mic night. *It was pure emotion.* For as long as I can remember, in its purest form, that's what music has been for me. Singing has put me in touch with emotions buried so deep within me, through all the years I believed I wasn't worthy of having them.

At the time, when I took to the improvised stage of the Pink Bean, I didn't see it as a big transitional moment in my life—I just wanted to sing a song—but in hindsight, it was. It was me communicating my emotions. My joy at being with Caitlin. At finding a home with the women who frequent the Pink Bean. At finding my true self somewhere in the ruins of my negative self-image.

Because of that moment, I've decided to take Kristin up on her offer to sing one Friday a month at the Pink Bean. I've had a lot of coaxing from Caitlin and Eva, of course. But my biggest fan, as always, has been my sister. I wish she could be here tonight. It would be difficult for her to come, but I believe that one Friday in the near future, she will. I will bring her here. I will have her sit in the audience and watch me. Bea will listen to her sister sing and hear what is possible, even for us Greenwood girls.

It was Declan who introduced me to a friend of his who plays the guitar. Jimmy is a skinny, pale man with dark curly hair and the longest fingers I've ever seen on a human being. For tonight, we've practiced five songs.

I wish Kristin would get a liquor license for the Pink Bean, so I could have a sip of something to take the edge off before I go on. Before we arrived, Caitlin took me to dinner, but I couldn't swallow one single bite. Even though I kept repeating my new mantra in my head: music is emotion. Nothing less. Nothing more. Yet, it still feels as though I'm about to give a big piece of myself on that stage.

Jimmy is testing the equipment he brought in earlier. Our set-up is the most basic you can have. Two microphones, an acoustic guitar and a small amplifier. That's it. Still, it feels like so much more than that night I first sang here. I'm glad to have Jimmy here with me. It stops me from feeling so on display, so naked.

Before I take my place behind the microphone, I look into the audience. It's a good turnout and everyone is here. Micky and Robin are chattering the way they always do. Sheryl is working the room, making people feel at home and relaxed. Kristin is talking to Alyssa behind the counter, telling her not to steam any milk during my performance. Martha and Amber are sitting at a table, chatting discreetly, their public demeanor always so controlled—quite the opposite of Micky and Robin. Eva, Declan and a few friends are grouped around a table. Zoya and two women I don't know sit at the table next to them. And right next to the stage, stands Caitlin.

Caitlin, whom I introduced to my parents only a few weeks after we started going out. Caitlin who pushed me to sing in public for the first time. Caitlin who brought me out of my shell with her patience and wisdom and life experience.

"I love you," she mouths. But she doesn't even have to say it anymore. I know it. I feel it every single day. Without her, I wouldn't be about to launch into my first song tonight. I would still believe there was something wrong with me for not being able to fully give myself to another person in certain circumstances. Despite all the theories I teach as part of my job, deep down, I would still believe I wasn't good enough for the kind of love she gives me every day. So, tonight, I will sing for her. Every note I push out of my mouth and every breath that will leave my lungs will be for her. For her belief in me. For the me she saw when I was too blind to see myself.

I wink at her, then look back at the crowd. I introduce myself and Jimmy, then say, "This song is dedicated to my partner Caitlin. For those of you who don't know her, she's that demure wallflower standing to my right." I turn to her, a big smile on my face. "I love you."

Jimmy and I have practiced a slower, fully acoustic version of Annie Lennox's "Little Bird" as an opening song. I sing it without thinking of anything and just let the emotion within me come out. I ignore my inner critic and just sing. I let it all go and when I get to take a little breather when Jimmy sings some *ooh-oohs* for backing vocals, I look into the audience, and I feel their energy. I feel their emotion coming back to me, and it spurs me on for a big finale, just letting everything go, and not caring about how I got here and the person I used to be. This is me now and now is all that matters.

When the song ends and Jimmy and I bask in the enthusiastic round of applause we receive, I look to my right. Caitlin is still there. Her lips are split into the widest smile. I look at her and I don't know what the future holds for us. All I know is that, because of her, so much has changed already.

ACKNOWLEDGEMENTS

I've been at this for a while now, but I still can't explain why writing some books is such utter joy and some need to be painfully bled from my fingertips onto the screen (or page). This one, however, came gushing out of me during the last four weeks of 2016, and it was such a month of pure elation.

I've relished every minute of writing this book, perhaps because I was in familiar territory with the May/December theme, or because I was writing in first person (my preferred point of view), or perhaps because I could finally put the difficulties between book one and three in a series behind me. I don't really know, but I do know that in Josephine Greenwood I created a character in which I could project a lot of my own doubts and fears about my body.

Despite my wife telling me I'm gorgeous every single day, I didn't grow up believing the way I looked would ever do. First as a tomboy with no real inclinations toward showing many outward signs of femininity; later as a woman who would stand in front of the mirror asking herself out loud: who could ever love this?

I'm guessing that's why, despite all our shortcomings and insecurities, Josephine and I fell in love with Caitlin simultaneously. And we both realized how the love of a good woman can help tremendously toward realizing your own worth.

I've been fortunate enough to have met that woman sixteen years ago, at the time when I needed saving from my thoughts of gloom the most. Prone to hyperbole as I am, it's nothing but the simple truth that without my wife's support throughout every single one of those sixteen years, throughout all the highs and very low lows, I would not be writing this as a note in my fourteenth full-length novel.

This lesfic journey has put me into contact with a bunch of wonderful people, and none more so than my beta reader Carrie. Thank you, Carrie, and once you get rid of that president we'll come visit you and talk about lesfic for days on end.

I've worked with quite a few editors over the course of these fourteen books and there's only one who manages to strike the perfect balance between constructive criticism and jokey comments. It's a delicate feat that only my friend and trusted editor Cheyenne Blue knows how to pull off.

As always, I must thank my Launch Team. It's a true privilege to have such a bunch of loyal readers in my corner who help make my books better and help me become a better writer in the process.

Most of all, Dear Reader, I owe gratitude to you and your continued support. Nothing in my life has ever made me feel more truly like myself than writing. I have screwed up a lot of things in my life, and I still do, but there's such comfort in waking up in the morning and knowing that I'm about to do what I love most in the world: making up lesbian love stories. Thanks to you, I get to do this for a living—and I get to feel good about myself on a daily basis.

Thank you.

ABOUT THE AUTHOR

Harper Bliss is the author of the novels *Beneath the Surface, In the Distance There Is Light, The Road to You, Seasons of Love,* and *At the Water's Edge,* the *High Rise* series, the *French Kissing* serial and several other lesbian erotica and romance titles. She is the co-founder of Ladylit Publishing, an independent press focusing on lesbian fiction. Harper is currently on a digital nomad adventure around the world with her wife Caroline.

Harper loves hearing from readers and if you'd like to drop her a note you can do so via harperbliss@gmail.com

Website: www.harperbliss.com
Facebook: facebook.com/HarperBliss
Twitter: twitter.com/HarperBliss